ABSTRACT: BOLD BLACK

A CRIME STORY WITH AN ARTISTIC TWIST

SCOTT PRICE

Abstract: Bold Black: A Crime Story With An Artistic Twist
Published by Finish Line Publishing
Denver, CO

ISBN: 978-0-578-82805-3
FICTION / Mystery & Detective / Amateur Sleuth

Abstract: Bold Black is a work of fiction. Any references to people, places or things are fictitious.

Cover and layout by Wolf Design and Marketing
Cover art by Scott Price

DEDICATION

To readers everywhere. Thank you. Keep reading. Enjoy.

ONE

SHE FINISHED HER RUN on the beach. It was warm outside but not yet hot like it would be. She felt good. She felt fit. Running along the edge of the water and over the occasional rises of the uneven dunes helped keep her legs trim. It was also a good escape for her mind. She stopped when she reached the deck and stretched easily, warming down. After a few stretches, she noticed the rear sliding doors that opened onto the deck, looking out to the sand and sea, were open. She came inside. The house, their beach escape place, was quiet. She hadn't seen him outside as she returned the same way that she had started out, and not on the deck while she warmed down. Standing in her great room, sweating, her breath still exercise labored, there was no one in sight. The adjacent large modern kitchen space was empty. She walked toward the master bedroom wing. Her mind was weighing whether to pull off her running halter-top and hit the shower first or just go jump into the small pool that they had built just off the deck. He liked them to rinse first, a habit he claimed came from years of swim team ritual. She liked to shed her running top and tight triathlon-type bottom that she enjoyed running in at the seclusion of the beach and feel the water of the pool envelope her from her toes to her head. It was an all-enveloping feeling, instead of the shower stream hitting the top of her head then cascading over the rest of her. And if she showered first, she still wanted that dunk in the pool. She would walk through the house naked trailing water on the floor. It didn't hurt the floor. They had remodeled the place, and it had stone tile and rugged wood flooring meant to withstand the inevitable nature of being on the beach. It was a little untidy for him, the trail of water, but he wouldn't complain as long as he saw it and didn't slip on it if he hadn't been paying attention. It was a small matter, but she knew it was there.

He wasn't in the bedroom. Her breathing was normal now. She paused and listened for a clue to where he might be. She was ready for the pool. She headed through the great room toward the outside again. The open doors prodded her attention. Leaving doors wide open is something he would do if he were in the vicinity. If he were inside, the roll of breeze bearing sea scent brought the great nature of the setting right to his lap. If he were outside, well, it was his nature to keep a part of his awareness on minding the house, keeping a fraction of an eye on matters, so nothing would go awry. She decided on a very short postponement of being ensconced in the water. She walked past the rooms they used as offices, even though this place was a retreat from full-fledged work. She called out his name to the end of the hall. She walked its length, took hold of the handle to the door at the end, and opened it. Both cars were in the garage. The one they drove here in from the city and the utility vehicle that they kept here at the house for taking their houseguests and themselves into the dunes for picnics and other outings. The garage was silent.

She was starting to feel that something isn't right feeling. She ran back through the house, looking in every room. She went out on the deck and scanned what she could see, sand and water. She ran all the way around the house. No sign. With the knotted feeling of something wrong starting to darken over her like a storm cloud, she traced the general path of their favorite walking areas through the dunes. No good. As twilight gathered, so did that terrible feeling known to everyone who has, even for a brief time, been unable to find their dog, child, cat, or loved one.

Then the wave of panic washed in. Where is he? Where is he? What has happened? Where, what, where? She wrestled to get control. Sit by the phone? Run through the dunes? Take the phone and run through the bushy growth bordering the sand? She did what so many do, convincing herself that wanting him to show up was an action equal to anything else that might be done. But the mental trick of calming herself this way wore off quickly. Now she was afraid, and, and … she didn't know what to do.

The evening, then the night, passed with an agony of slowness. You don't really sleep, just nod off from exhaustion eventually, only to awake with the harsh reality before you. With dawn came those rays of hope of some news, of a change in the situation, with hope for better. But those rays of hope dissolved as daylight rolled on in its clarity.

She called the police.

TWO

IT WAS MIDDAY, and it was hot. The heat shimmered above the sand and highlighted the sparkle at the tips of the small waves that lapped at the shore. The promise of cool relief awaited there in the water, once the crossing of the burning sand had been negotiated.

I was gazing out over the heated foreground topped by the azure water of the ocean, soaking in the reflected heat, savoring the warmth and letting it comfort me. I had little more than an hour until a new client was coming to see me. She had a problem. I'm good at unraveling problems. I was already turning over and over in my mind her problem—the sudden disappearance of her husband, vanished into thin air, or, perhaps, into the murky depths of the ocean waters that I was gazing upon. This is a mystery I am going to unravel. I was kind of squinting, my eyes scrunched in that 'I am really thinking hard about this' way when, just in the corner of my right eye there was a movement, and it caught my attention.

I shifted slightly and let my eye take it in. Long shapely

legs. The splash of blue and gold tied stylishly around her hips. The legs hadn't been in the Florida sun for too much time yet. Not pale, not pasty, nothing so noticeable as a just deplaned or de-car-ed northern immigrant mushing through the sand eager to soak up the rejuvenating glow of the sun magnified by the golden sand, buffered by the azure sea that blended into the openness of the blue sky. No, these legs had already experienced the glow but promised to become so much more with time. There are many, many beautiful people to be found on the shore. This one was stunning. Now it wasn't just a portion of my eye noticing. She had my full attention. She stood for a moment gazing out to the water, a canvas tote bag hanging at her side from one hand. The other held a straw hat that she was using, held just above her head, to shield her eyes as she took in the view. She bent over and pulled a colorful beach blanket from the tote. She snapped it horizontally over the spot she had chosen and it settled lightly to the sand. She sat down, put her hat over her golden hair, pulled her knees up to her chest and sat, gazing again out to sea.

Whew.

I hadn't realized how intently I had been watching until her pose allowed me to sit back and relax as well. As I began to breathe more regularly again—I know I hadn't been holding my breath, but somehow shallow breathing had taken over there for a bit. I also looked around. I noticed several other fellows who seemed to be giving up forward leans in their chairs, moving into the backrests, with smiles emerging. I smiled too.

Another thing I noticed was that the sounds on the deck had emerged again. The clink of glass and dish, various conversations, the scuff of sandals on the cedar planking. I knew it hadn't actually gotten silent for those moments, but I also knew that it had for those of us doing the watching on the beach. A momentary thought of what action might be taken—this was someone that might be worth pursuing—bounded through my head, but it was fleeting for my head was too wrapped around the disappearance, and I was back to thinking about how I was going to investigate this mystery that I was being brought into, a matter that, by its nature, could contain some unpleasantness.

I paid for the coffee that I had been drinking, left the beachside bar deck, and headed to my office. It was a short and sunny walk. My office, my base of operations, is right here on the beach as well. Housed in a building I purchased and renovated is my gallery, my work studio, and my home. I am an artist, a painter. Approaching the gallery, I could already see through the large front windows the splashes of color on the walls that my style is known for. I was pleased to see that there were several people in the gallery looking at paintings, and that my gallery manager Cathy, doing a job that she's good at, was talking with two of them.

Browsing is great. People should go into art galleries and just look, see if something leaps out at them. When I walk into a gallery sometimes the colors just fly at me. That's the experience I love to have. Sometimes it happens with more subtlety. The images just work themselves into my consciousness. That experience can be gratifying too. I've watched as people move through, tilting their heads, stepping closer, then stepping back, as they look at certain pieces. Then they'll look back to something they've already passed, and you know that piece is working its way into their head or heart. When they actually walk back to a piece, walk away, look back, walk back, then, it's sure they've seen something, been touched somehow. Still, even after this dance of attraction, uncertainty, needing another look, most often nothing comes of it. That's okay. It stimulated them for a few moments. Made them think, consider. Maybe it even made them count the numbers in their checkbook, the limit on the credit card available, the 'purchase decision'. Enough lookers do decide to purchase to make it worthwhile for me. But even if they just look, that makes it worthwhile too, there's hope that they take a positive response away with them.

I walked through the show space. Cathy was in a discussion, and I didn't approach. She either didn't see me or didn't decide to acknowledge me. I went into the area that is my office. I like the grouping of my areas. Gallery, for selling the work, studio, where I do most of my painting, office, for keeping track of things and handling other business, and home up above. But, of course, the entire place feels like home. But now I needed to think. That's what I had started out to do on the deck, until I got distracted by the sights on the beach. Sometimes it worked very well staring out at the ocean swells. Sometimes it created a surrounding peace that let my mind turn over what I knew, what I didn't know but needed to know, how the pieces might fit together. Sometimes it didn't work, particularly when the rise and fall of non-ocean swells came into view.

A new client is coming to see me. She had stopped in yesterday, but I wasn't there. Cathy told me she had walked in, a little uncertain, probably about whether she was in the right place. She had been told about me by someone who knew me, that's how I get this type of client, and she knew I was a painter too, but she didn't know quite what that meant or what to expect. I have two client lists, those that purchase my paintings and those who enlist my investigator services. And there is intertwining. Cathy had sized her up, of course, and could tell the artwork wasn't the draw for her, so gave her a smile, a 'good-morning', and a 'how can we help you?' It took only a moment to get that she wanted to talk to me about the other business I did, the business that had started because 'exploring things' was something that fit for me, was something I can do. Prowling around is sometimes more like it. Finding out things. Finding out what happened, who was involved, and, more times than not, why. I'm good at investigating, piecing it together. It takes work, but I like it. Oftentimes it is difficult for a new client to understand the relationship—painter, investigator, artist, and detective. I get it though. The act of composing new artwork, infusing it with feeling, structure, and color feels very compatible with discerning the elements of a problem, the unknown, analyzing the likely scenarios of what happened, then pursuing some arrangement of the known and the unknown that will lead to solving a mystery. Ah yes, orderly, maybe even scientific-sounding. Yeah, mostly not. Mostly it's try, try, try and try some more. Sometimes brilliant things appear. Sometimes you just stumble in the right door. But, that's part of the adventure, spurring creativity.

This investigative work had started, as a business, in school. I was pretty sure I wanted to paint, to create works of art. I was also pretty sure that I would find acceptance, perhaps acclaim, and that I would 'do well' at it. I couldn't be quite as sure when all this would fall into place, but it would. However, in the meantime, I found that the imagination that made me think the art would turn out all right and made me believe I could create it in the first place, led me into some situations that are best described as involving 'intrigue'.

I cast about for odd jobs that would contribute some pocket money and still leave me enough free time to paint. Of course, given youth and an inclination for artistic expression, the exact amount of free time necessary was not predictable, so flexibility was essential. An opportunity presented itself in the form of an 'investigative agency'. It was an ad in the paper. When I called and expressed interest, they said to come in, and we'd talk it over. So I did. It was a type of detective agency. Their primary work was researching—going to the county and paging through records, scanning microfiche, and as the world evolved, searching through computer records. County records, city records, wherever background might be found, or, where a hint might lead to coaxing some gossip or hearsay or unwritten information out of someone somewhere. It was mostly unexciting, but I learned valuable things. I learned how to search out information and how to reason, or to speculate, what the records didn't actually say, but could be hinting at. More importantly, I learned what really goes on in the background, in expectedly *normal* subdivision streets, in homes, in offices, in bars and restaurants, and in every place where one person mingles with another. A lot of unexpected things happen in those expectedly *normal* places, things that sometimes seemed stranger than the things that happened in back streets and in dark places where you figured they would be happening. Things happened in both those *normal* places and in those dark places that sense could be made of only to someone who experienced them enough to come to accept the unexpected as normal.

It turned out I was quite good at it. I was able to make the leap from the black and white of the ordinary printed, scanned and computed words to the colorations of what the words represented, the stories they intimated, the rationales for the actions that could have happened, and often did happen. The tricky part was my aversion to fixed hours, since the places where records are kept hold to a fairly rigid schedule of hours of operation. The *regular* business day. That went against my grain more than I thought it would.

I liked the off hours. I liked the night. The warm darkness embraced me. The feeling that no one else could see. That meant that freedom was at hand, to do what I wanted where I wanted. To see what was to be seen. To remain undetected myself.

The agency learned that I could do a pretty good job when the hours coincided with my preferred hours of operation. That led to the occasional research project that relied less on records research and more on observation of matters occurring in real time. With this, my second and often paralleling career truly embarked.

And so it was this second pursuit that had brought this new client to me. Her name is Vickie Reeves. Her disappeared husband is James Reeves. She was ten, maybe fifteen, years older than me. She was in shape, a slightly athletic look, with nice curves at the waist and hip and that little extra heft to her chest that I couldn't help but notice. She had auburn hair and, although it wasn't much in evidence, when she did smile just a little, her smile had a twist of mischievousness that said to me, 'do you think you can handle me?'. Was this a competitive personality trait, or something else? We sat, and talked, and over the course of about twenty minutes, she told me of the sudden disappearance of her husband.

She: "I like your paintings. Bold."

Me: "Thank you."

She: "But you also do investigations?"

Me: "Yes, the mental aspect is similar."

She: "I see. So do you think you can help me? He's been missing for three days now."

Me: "Yes, I can at least help sort out the situation."

She: "He just vanished from our get-away house at the beach. It's a little remote, there's not much around, nothing close. The cars are still in the garage. But, he's gone."

Me: "And you've called the police?"

She: "Yes, they came out, looked around, searched the shoreline for awhile."

Me: "And you think they're looking into it?"

Her answer was a sideways tilt of her head, the tilt that speaks 'I guess so'.

We called the lead investigator. There wasn't much to report. It seemed to me that there wasn't much importance attached to the case from their perspective. When we hung up, she looked at me.

"Not very encouraging," I said.

She just nodded sadly, her eyes falling to the floor.

Was it possible she knew more? Maybe she had something to do with it. He could have planned it, to run off with someone else. He might have had something happen at the wrong time while swimming in the ocean, or perhaps a watery demise had been planned. Or, perhaps, he might have been abducted. For a business reason? Kidnapped for ransom? No demand had been forthcoming, yet. Maybe, since she had the looks for it, she had gotten tired of her husband and was looking for, no, already had, a new young paramour. She was attractive, and that was something I found myself thinking about. She was well off enough, at least it seemed so, with the get-away beach house and her dress and manner. Had she had help, whatever the method of disappearance? Was it for an inheritance? For insurance? For revenge? I was seeing a canvas in front of me with bold slashes of red and black on top of a blue-green horizon that might represent water. I needed to control my imagination, harness the creative force, and start composing an image to at least work from.

I looked right at her. She had come to me when it seemed the police weren't doing enough. And she had a nice smile, even if it seemed a little enigmatic. She wasn't smiling much though. I decided I liked her and was leaning toward accepting the story at face value.

Thinking about this, considering what I thought might be so and what might not be, and strategizing on what actions to be employed to help me understand the situation best is what had distracted me from the more enjoyable distraction I had been witnessing on the beach. And now it's time to act.

THREE

I WANTED TO SEE the place of the disappearance for myself. I drove south out of San Isabel, down the coast. I loved this drive, through the dunes and the mid-high growth of bushes that at times boxed the road in, at times opened up to a scattered landscape pattern spread across the sandy ground. Sometimes the ocean was in view, and sometimes it dipped away out of sight. The wonderful smell of saltwater baked in the heat was always present. The Reeves's had a beach house down the shore a ways, and that's where I was headed, to see what I could learn, if I could learn, first hand from the scene of the vanished husband. She and her husband came up to the house occasionally, a getaway place from the big Miami metropolis on the opposite coast. They had been there four days this time, when her husband had disappeared. They liked to walk along the shore, swim, read, putter, just take it easy, or at least easier, when they came here. He often brought some work along, but not for full-time attention. They shared the enjoyment of the place, so it was unusual to go through most of the day without seeing one another numerous times unless one of them decided to go into town.

I turned off the main road at the spot Vickie had described for me. Since I was looking for it, it could be noticed, but if you weren't looking for it, it looked like most of the rest of the area. There was nothing that would draw someone this way, the little-used indentation that passed for a roadway not appearing to go anywhere. Now I was angling closer toward the ocean. After about five hundred yards, the road changed direction, running parallel to the shore. I knew the shore was there even though it wasn't visible from the road past the rising dunes. Soon came her described driveway, they were few and far in-between, and soon the driveway led to the house. It was large, beautifully set among the rises of sand and bush. You could tell just approaching it that it had spectacular views over the beach to the ocean. Quite a getaway place.

The exterior of cedar weathered to worn gray looked well maintained. The driveway split, one part heading for the multiple doored garage toward one end of the house. The other leg of the drive curled toward a parking and turnaround area fronting the entry. The weathered cedar stood in contrast to the cut-glass adornments on either side, which rounded above an imposing antiqued copper door. I rang the bell.

Vickie answered and ushered me in. The approach to the house hinted at what the interior sumptuously revealed. Magnificent ocean vistas met every step we took. In my detective and painter pursuits, I'd been in many magnificent properties and seen many fantastic views, but no matter how many I saw, a new one always brought with it a sense of awe at the abundant and varied magnificence of nature. Here it was before us.

"This is spectacular."

My eyes took in more than the words expressed.

"It is usually a joy to see this view, thank you. For the last few days, it's been hard to focus on it."

She spoke softly. I heard the discouragement.

"I understand."

"Would you like to go out on the deck or talk inside?"

The deck was my choice. In good times, it's hard to imagine a better place to converse, to share, to absorb the warmth, to take in the fragrance of the seawater. In harder times it can offer a place for reflection, and often there is comfort in that. The deck at my place is a favorite roost. We'll see if this one comes with any insight.

We sat in comfortable chairs. The view was spectacular. The mood was somber. She began by recounting the evening he went missing. I had heard this before, but it seemed the way she needed to tell it. At first, she thought he was just wandering somewhere. Then the realization that something was wrong. Then getting through that night. When no word or encouragement of any kind appeared, she called the police. She had explained all of this to them. It wasn't until they had surveyed the property that it was pointed out to her that there was damage around the lock to one of the rear doors.

Had she known about this?

Had this happened as part of the disappearance?

She hadn't noticed it, and no, it wasn't like that before.

Was anything missing, that is, any property missing?

Well, no, she didn't think so, but she hadn't really been aware it was a possibility.

Please look around now and see what you notice, or don't notice.

So, she did. She walked around the house, but nothing appeared to be out of place, and nothing seemed to be missing. The place was beautiful, but it wasn't their main home, so there weren't things of real value generally kept here. The furnishings were nice. Sound systems, computer, televisions. But nothing seemed to be missing. Even after the police left, she continued to try to look at the interior in that way, is something missing? What am I not seeing? But, there were no gaps, no spaces that should have been filled that weren't.

It had been only a few days, but the police had nothing to report. She felt that it wasn't that important to them either. That's why she came to me.

James Reeves was a businessman. Banking, investments. She knew what he did, although not in great detail. He left for work, came home. They talked about it a little, she always wanted to know more, he always kept it general. He occasionally had meetings. He occasionally went away on business, but not long trips.

He, or they, had a boat. He liked it more than she did. But it was fun to occasionally go out for a few hours. He, they, kept it docked at a yacht club. Yes, in Miami.

She gave me a description of the boat. We talked about the yacht club. She described exactly where it was docked, how they would park and the club help, mostly young people working part time, would help get their things onto the boat, picnic things, a bag or two, never all that much, they were just going for a short outing.

She just didn't know why this had happened. There weren't problems with them. There weren't problems with money. Everything seemed fine. Everything had been normal for them. She didn't know what to do.

As I listened to her, I also took in the murmur of the surf. I wasn't sure whether I was hearing an undercurrent of things unsaid, of things unknown.

FOUR

I LEFT MRS. REEVES, drove a short distance, then stopped, and wrote out some notes of our meeting, adding these to the notes I had made after she first came to see me. Some things were clear, but not many. It could be a kidnapping. It could be a planned disappearance. It didn't add up to being a result of a confrontation related to the break-in. There had been no contact, no ransom, or other demand call, so a straight kidnapping didn't add up. It seemed a difficult place and circumstance to stage a disappearance, in order to walk out on her. But then again, out at the shore, he could have had someone waiting to pick him up. So that was a possibility.

At a meeting I preferred to listen, think, and absorb, at least in initial meetings. Observing details is part of artistic tradition. The ability to do this served me well in both art and investigation. But it was also my habit to do what I was doing now. I had gone only a quarter-mile away, and there was a widening of the road margin where it was easy to pull over. The spot had a view of the water and I looked out at it for a handful of beats, then pulled out a small spiral notebook and wrote my impressions. Some of it was fact. Some of it was impressions. You had to have the facts, but you'd know nothing without the impressions. Recalling the information provided, gleaned or surmised after the moment helped cement the event for me. Writing it down helped too. I headed home knowing that during the drive, the discussion and the event would get turned over, get brain massaged—and impression massaged.

Back in San Isabel I sat down in my studio, and tried to think. First, I thought about whether a beer, some wine or a drink might help me think. But, I knew that would help me think about some things but not about this. I walked around my office, but couldn't find the right focus.

Next, I thought about whether doing some painting would help me think. Often creative thought, occasionally even inspiration, would come when deliberate thought on a matter was set to the side, with just the notion that something needed to be allowed to seep into my consciousness. It worked best when there was a motivation. A color I wanted to explore, for instance. In the doing of that I could become immersed in the color, in the emotions that arose or be invigorated by the creativity that welled out of the expression of paint color on canvas. Sometimes it resulted in a work that felt real-ized, expressing feelings about life, about the work, about dreams. Sometimes the effort left room for other creativity to emerge—that glimmer of insight into the matter set aside.

I looked at a couple of canvases I had set up. I like to work big, not the end of the last abstract phase, Rauschenberg-big, room sized big, no. My works are five foot by six foot on the small side, six by eight, eight by eight. Big enough for free, bold expression. The canvases I was looking at represented ideas that were forming, the stirrings and emotions that rose inside me, that would become a driving force that had to be depicted, at least that would be the best result. Sometimes I had to step back and wait for the power to rise again. I decided I needed a glass of wine.

I strolled absentmindedly around my lair for just a little bit longer, then decided the way to go was to go out front, onto the street, to walk a bit, in search of the right tonic.

This isn't a big town. A little bit touristy, a little bit beach-goers, and a little bit laid back residents. We have some nice restaurants, ranging from burgers and beers to trendy seafood places. And we have a good ice cream shop. What more fun can you have? I've enjoyed ice cream shops, or their equivalent, around the world. France, Italy, glace, gelato. Pick a favorite. My favorite? Well, it revolves. Strawberry soothes in a hot atmosphere. Chocolate—but of course. Vanilla is great at the right time. Currently, coffee, or mocha if I can find it, rules the day. The town is friendly, comfortable, and you can't beat the surroundings.

The decision to walk was a good one and after about twenty-five minutes of strolling, my mind was clearer and the required path was beginning to show itself. When I got back home, I was ready to get down to business. I got out the notes I had made after leaving Vickie. I still liked her and hadn't come up with any good reason not to take this on. There was something else, and I had known it from our first meeting. She reminded me very much of someone, and that memory made me want to help her. When we met, I was struck by how much she looked like an art teacher I worked with one summer. I was already studying painting but wanted more and it hadn't been difficult to locate someone to give private instruction. Vickie looked very much like Connie, and the age difference was about the same as it had been with her. Connie's studio was in a detached one-car garage at the rear of her small older house, in a revitalizing neighborhood. Her VW Beetle got parked alongside the garage, not in it. I found her ad for instruction in the back of a local weekly, we met and hit it off.

We started meeting to paint on a MWF schedule, for a couple hours. We would start mid-morning, talk about techniques, composition and color theory. We both would paint some then do mutual criticism. It was stimulating. We could paint for only a few minutes and want to question and discuss what we were doing. We could paint for an hour or more before wanting to draw back and discuss how we felt about what we were producing. The back and forth pointing to successes and flaws was immediately rewarding when it was good and beneficial when revisions were obviously necessary. All the criticism was delivered in a supportive way so mistakes or misdirection wasn't negative, it was process to move to better work. It was growth. It was invigorating.

Since it was summer and warm, we painted mostly just outside her garage studio in the small but lovely treed and flowering yard area. Our subjects weren't plein air strictly, it was just comfortable outdoors. My preferred outfit for painting was then and remains shorts and t-shirt with canvas type shoes, like skate shoes, to cover my feet because when I get going at times the paint can fly. Her outfits varied more than mine. Mostly shorts, of varying degrees of shortness. Her choices for tops included t-shirts too, but she had some choices that were sometimes distracting. She had several tops that were similar to a popular style of tank tops but more open and might better be likened to old man undershirts. The image is apparent to most. The intriguing part, when worn by a woman, is the open side area under the arms. Lots of women wear this top with some form of tube top, and the outfit appears comfortable…and airy.

After a few weeks of working on painting together, we had become pretty comfortable with each other. One day started off warm and progressed quickly to quite hot. She was wearing one of these intriguing open-sided arrangements. After some painting and then some shared critical discourse she mentioned that the heat was as forecast and that she had made some iced tea in anticipation and would I like some. Sure, I said. It was in the house and she went to get it. My offered help was turned down.

I played with my painting for a few dabs with my brushes, and she was back and set down a pitcher on a table we used to hold some of our working supplies. She held out a filled glass to me. I accepted, with thanks and, looking into her face, did a slight mimic of the big grin she had on hers. I lifted the glass to drink, and she turned to her easel. I noticed something. The open-sided top she was wearing was white. Underneath it had been a blue tube top. I had noticed. My eyes had drifted to that view a few times. The blue under the white wasn't there anymore. I held the glass to my lips, but I was looking over the rim. Connie raised her hand and brush to her canvas and I was treated to that delightful visage of swelled flesh through the open-sided top. I slowly lowered the glass. We painted on our own projects for awhile. My concentration had been affected. I had noticed her occasional bra-less look in t-shirts before and liked what was suggested. This was two steps beyond. She put down her brush, assessed the work on her canvas, then looked over at me. 'Are you cooler now?' Ten different replies raced through my head. 'Not so much, are you?' was the reply that came out. She laughed lightly, with a slight backward head tilt. I'm convinced she blushed slightly.

Connie turned and went into the studio. I stood for a moment, said to myself this is a 'if you're gonna shoot, shoot, don't talk' moment, put down my brush and went into the studio. She was fiddling with something on a workbench. I walked up close to her. 'I couldn't help but notice how lovely you are under your shirt.' Direct. It would be fly or crash. Her 'yeah, what else have you got look' told me I needed more. 'I want to paint you in the nude.' Her smile continued. One beat. Then she said, 'does that mean you'll be nude…or me?' A touch of humor was a positive response. 'Yes' I said. Her head went back into that slight tilt again, with a big smiled laugh. She took hold of the bottom of her top and lifted it over her head. No more painting was done that day.

The summer passed too quickly. We painted and constructively cross criticized, and shed our clothes often. With the start of a new school year, our obligations increased, and we didn't have the idyllic time of the summer. I started doing more and more investigation work and she took on more artist representation. We still saw each other, but far less frequently. We still do.

Vickie stimulated my memory of my fondness for that summer and Connie. I liked the feeling. It gave me a very positive outlook. So that was it. I liked Vickie, and she needed help. I'm going to do it. There didn't seem to be any better likely starting place than where Vickie said Mr. Reeves was headquartered out of—Miami.

FIVE

ON ANY GIVEN MORNING I'm moved to either start some coffee or splash my hair into decent enough shape to go to Common Bean, a great little coffee shop just off the beach. Sometimes the deciding factor is whether I have any croissants or pastry around. Sometimes it's the weather. Some mornings it's great to go out, order coffee and a treat and watch the girls as they head for a morning of sun and sand, or, just watch as the locals head to their posts. Some mornings, when it's cloudy and not perfect for bikini gazing, it's still great to be out and to bask in the atmospheric richness that permeates the still air while the horizon is blurred where water and sky merge into one. But, this morning it would be fire up the home coffee machine, and some fresh berries would do just fine for the treat.

I paged through the paper with the first cup. Mostly just turning the pages, scanning for anything interesting, or, less likely, informative. Of course, I get my world information from all the sources available, not just a newspaper. The paper is good for really local happenings. Besides, I just it enjoy it, a little throwback, I know, but that's how it is. With the second cup I packed a bag, shorts and polo's, with just one pair of khakis in case long pants were needed. Driving was easiest for this trip. I didn't know exactly what areas I'd be poking around in. Also, I like the thinking time behind the wheel. Driving anywhere near the coast filled me with good spirits, smelling the sea air, the occasional glimpses of waster past the sand and scrub, the open sky.

The transition from open road to city outskirts, then suburbs, is bittersweet. The open road is just that, open. The mind flirts with images of anything-can-happen, all dreams can come true, all cares are nothing when viewed against the wide-open sky. The flirtations of the mind get replaced, without being knowingly dismissed, with intensifying attention paid to routes, destinations, and traffic. At some point you are navigating the great metropolis and concentrating on the pulses of information that come at you with increasing speed and intensity. Successfully managing this metropolis endeavor is rewarding in a far different way than the airy enrapture of more open spaces.

I like Miami. It's vibrant. It is colorful. It's so international now it makes you feel as if you could be in an exotic foreign place, but, it is also very US of A, which is a great combination. Colorful people. Colorful streetscapes. The beauty of sun and sand, and the people that like to soak it up. Ah yes, there are beauties to behold here.

I very much like my more laid back lifestyle at home, but it's great to enjoy the vibrancy of a high-octane metro center.

There are times when it is a fabulous getaway—to hit the clubs, restaurants, and nightspots. I have my favorites, and I like to check out the new spots. Sometimes it's fun to do the town with some local friends. Sometimes it's fun just to see what new friends might be encountered. When I'm here for these adventures I prepare a little differently than when it's a 'business' trip.

Once I entered the firm bounds of the city, I made my way to my headquarters for this trip, a comfortable and welcoming travel accommodation despite the modern hallmarks of corporate influenced visions of the roadside hostelry.

Next, I made my way to the Harbor Bay Yacht Club. I wonder which came first, yacht clubs or golf county clubs? Either way, they often feel very much the same. A bit elitist, a bit put-off-ish—Are you sure you belong here? If you didn't *feel* that you *did* belong, a person certainly could feel trepidation approaching one or the other. I'd bet that at least half of the people that did belong liked belonging because they weren't sure they did belong, but paying the dues at least let them in the doors.

Well, I knew that feeling, but happily, or at least usefully, I had gotten over it. Although I still remembered it. Gaining success, and some recognition in painting had been a big help. Success helps you to feel that, well, I'm welcome here, because this is a success recognition place. Some practice at just walking through doors and feeling that you can deal with whatever approaches you helps too.

So it was with confidence that I parked my car and began walking through the beautifully landscaped and shaded parking area toward the club entrance. But halfway there I saw through a parting of the hedges lining the entrance approach, a walkway leading to the dock areas. Well, I thought, this might be a better approach than storming a fort where I didn't yet know the layout or what I was looking for.

The walkway to the moorings was wide, wide enough for two golf carts to pass if they encountered one another. I mused for just a moment about the golf club/ yacht club thing because of the notion of golf carts, but let it go. The walkway was smooth, densely packed fine gravel material, with hard edges of concrete, and with a coloration that looked neither like concrete nor the ground that bordered it, although calling it colored didn't describe it nearly well enough. It was more like patinaed, giving it an old, well-established look. It contributed to the well-kept and long-established look of the grounds, with landscaping extending outward from the hard borders holding the walkway in place. There was something here about the attention to detail that contributed to the sense of belonging of the place. The walkway could have been asphalt or concrete, but the fine gravel material dissipated heat better and made a better statement of sophistication. The dual materials of the walkway and the patinated concrete guiding it along was the kind of detail that said—'we're good'.

Before the walkway turned into the planks of the docks there was a small but ample multi-sided shack that was used to dispense towels and helpers. I thought it could also function as a guardhouse if need be. The shack appeared empty at the moment.

I walked on.

The docking area showed the same attention to detail. It was weathered and looked appropriate against the sea. It was weathered but not worn. The docks spread out into the harbor like fingers from many hands. There was quite a lineup of boats, waiting at rest for their pilots and their next rush into the challenge of the encompassing silvery tipped waves beyond the calm of the harbor. They ranged from large and flamboyant to merely expensively demure. There were all variety of motored boats and those gems of self-propulsion, the sailboats. Tall masts trailing their rigging spiked upward needling into the sky. There were models with vast windshields covered by sun protection that made them look like they were wearing huge opaque sunglasses. I drank in the overall effect of the scene, and this was a scene that really appealed to me, with a predominance of whites, in hulls and tops, and the whites were often set off with blue accents. There were some beiges and greens. There was the occasional burst of yellow. Then there was a personal favorite, the dabbed in highlight—red! All these colors literally floated on a marvelous blue canvas stretching to the horizon, where the blue continued, taking on a lighter hue than the blue in the foreground. There were subtle accents in this picture, as well. The occasional flag left to mambo on its own when the breeze prodded it into motion. There were glints of brass and steel. There were the sterns proud with their golden high-lighted titles—Luv 2 Sail, Beautiful Miss Deb, Le Express, Fun n the Sun. As I walked along, surveying this whole scene that I found so visually attractive, I realized that there was an added enchantment—the scene had its own auditory track.

There was the soft slap of surges of water against the hulls and against the mooring docks. There were sounds that you naturally recognize as watercraft related, the sometimes rhythmic sometimes staccato soft plink plink of one rigging component against a compatriot, singing out with a sway of the hull or the insistence of a burst of breeze. The soft groan of constraint from the tie lines and anchoring as the hulls of these buoyant vessels protest being held at rest against their will and signaled their willingness to venture into the azure sea for their next water test.

As I ventured along the docks I knew where to look, at least where to begin. When Mrs. Reeves told me about the yacht, I had followed up with 'where was it located? Did she have a picture?'. She did, and now I did. I had coaxed her to outline a map of where in the dock complex it was moored. Having a bit of knowledge going in was always useful. So I knew what I was looking for and where it should be found.

I found the boat at its berth. It was a marvelous sailing craft with a gleaming white hull and blue pinstripes. It was tethered fore and aft yet maintained its look of elegance. Its stern proclaimed, written in that same golden hand that I had seen so many other names, Sombreado.

I didn't know that word. Slumber, no. Some derivation of the Spanish sombra perhaps, shade or shadow?

I stood admiring the sailboat.

Then, I heard the approach of footsteps.

The footfalls were from a nice looking teenager. Boat shoes, shorts, polo shirt that had a Harbor Bay Y. C. logo on it. When I had passed the shack there was a signboard that said 'On duty today' with just one name posted—Josh. The confidence I have in myself is one thing. Outright lying is something else. You would think that someone in my situation would be good at lying. I have a really hard time lying. I can usually be creative when I find myself in that 'better come up with a good story to explain this' situation. Yet I never feel completely right at taking advantage of someone who might not deserve it—like a kid working at probably a first or part-time job. But I don't like to explain myself when I don't have to either. I took a shot.

"You're Josh, aren't you?"

So here we go, I'll be bullshitting a kid working part time or for the summer. It's not as rewarding as going against someone more knowledgeable.

"Hi, yes," he said.

"Hi, back."

It took only an instant for him to grasp that I had the look of belonging. He didn't start with who the hell are you? He just walked up to someone on his dock, during his tour of duty, and said, 'Hi.' I settled into casual.

"Nice day. Friend's boat. Fun to stand out here and take it in. How's your day going? Do you get a chance to go out some? This is a pretty nice boat, isn't it."

We spoke for only a short time. Josh was eager to be helpful. I left him behind with the same confident air. Okay, that went okay, I mused to myself. Sometimes getting by with stories and bullshit works better than other times.

I headed off the dock and back toward the club. Did I

need to broach the doors of the club? No, no need for that now. I turned toward the parking area. Did I learn anything?

My car was in the shade. I got out my notebook. I replayed the past bit of time in my head. What had I heard? Yes, I had heard it, but it didn't quite register just the right way.

Vickie Reeves referred to it as 'his' boat.

The kid said, "Mr. Hand had it out, for like…five days or so…, it's only been back for a day."

"Oh, I thought this was Mr. Reeves's boat."

"Oh, yes, it is."

"And Mr. Reeves usually sails with Mrs. Reeves. They usually show up and take right out. Not much talk, you know, small talk, how's it going. They're nice, but, just here, then on the boat. Then gone."

I wasn't completely sure where this was going when we were talking, so…

"But this time just Mr. Hand took it out?"

"Yes, he and Mr. Reeves have gone out together a couple times, and I've seen both of them sailing, and, well, he had the key…"

"Of course," I said although I really didn't know what was up, and didn't say so. I decided to learn if there was a routine that he might know about.

"Do they have dinner or drinks in the club when they come in?"

"No, I don't think so. I haven't helped them a lot, but I have brought one of the carts to them, they usually load up their stuff themselves, take it to their car and leave. Which is, of course, they are okay to do, that's how it works here."

"But, don't they go into the club, wind down, get a drink after a couple hours at sea?"

"Well, no, not from what I see, but, you know, I'm only part-time fill-in."

"Okay, well, thanks, it was nice of you to give me some time."

"Oh, sure, sir, that's why I'm here. Thank you. Well, better run."

"Yeah."

"Oh, say, just a question. The boat looks immaculate, having just been out. Did you do the cleanup?"

"Well, yeah, sure, that's what we do. But...well...it's kinda like you were asking, they don't have us do much for them. It's moored here, and we look after it in the normal way, walk by, yeah everything's okay way, but, they almost never have us do any servicing. Yeah, gas/oil, etc., but not cleaning or anything inside. It's just their way."

Their way. Vickie Reeves says his boat. Mr. Hand took it out. Just got back in. Mr. Reeves's been missing for a week.

"Uh, excuse me. Is there anything else...uh...I can help you with?"

Even replaying it in my head, I remembered how I was jerked back from trying to assimilate what I was learning.

"Uh, no, no, thanks. Oh, wait, we know Mr. and Mrs. Reeves, did any others usually go out?"

"Uh, there's them, I mean Mr. and Mrs. Reeves, but there's also the three others, Mr. Hand, Mr. Barton, and Mr. Cardenas. That's who just came in."

"Oh, of course, I should have known." I lied.

Recalling this conversation to myself, I thought I should

have asked if the three other Mr.'s dined or drank at the club. Should have. Darn.

SIX

I DECIDED TO do some sightseeing before having dinner. My prime spot is South Beach. It's a great district for walking around, only a few city blocks in size. By day there are the mansions and buildings, in all their restored art deco glory, not only the pastel-colored facades but also the designs, the decorative elements, the eyebrows over windows that create shade for the windows and visual interest in the shadows they cast. Another stylistic element is another window treatment, the porthole windows reminiscent of ocean liners. The buildings themselves, while multi-storied, are not huge things that block out the sun. I've heard the buildings in the district compared to Paris, and the summation is typically that the buildings are at a scale more friendly to humans.

This place is an international playground, and cultures from all over the world are represented. There are people to watch up and down the streets, in and out of shops, cafes, and other stops. There is the beach, big and wide with soft sand, perfect for walking, and, the people watching on the beach is even more fun than on the street. Fewer clothes. South Beach is filled with sights, sounds, smells, and scents. And then there is after dark. The buildings stay in place but their art deco designs, the ornamentation, the curved edges, when neon-lit, create a whole different vibe that is part pure romance, part otherworldly transport to another time, another era, and part amusement park. At night everything spills into the streets, from people to music—pulsing rhythms, driving beats, from Cuba and all the Caribe to NY/LA tech and hip hop, and then back again to Miami Sound Machine, the conga beat. What you see most often here is diversity and happiness. Some are living it, others are visiting it, but they all become entwined in the good life on Ocean Drive.

Ocean Drive is a colorful scene. The magnificent art deco buildings still suggest clandestine rendezvous and relations. Secrets kept and revealed. Promises and cash swapped for other valuables. Its old-time charm has been rapidly erod-ing, replaced by hustle-hustle bars serving margaritas by the gallon and buckets at a time of beer. It's still a gathering place but now more for visitors. Locals and old-timers have moved to more welcoming oases, like spots in Little Havana and other locally known haunts where charm still pervades. A real smile from an experienced waitress. An acknowledg-ing nod from the veteran behind the bar. No spritzing spray systems.

Contrary to the notion fed to visitors lined up six deep on the west side of Ocean Drive, the spritzing doesn't water down the drinks and allow you to consume more without effect. It's good that there is so little parking so that most imbibers must walk to get there or take taxis. And yet, for some in the know, there are still places to go.

Now it's time for dinner. I ducked into a smaller hotel I know with a bar and restaurant, and ate at the bar. Much easier for one. Fresh seafood. Another of the joys of shore living. They had a nice selection of wines, quite a few more choices than most these days and they weren't trying to become rich on each and every bottle they offered. It gave me the opportunity to select something that would be just right. I chose a terrific white wine, a Chablis. Umm, French. The wine was the color of soft golden sunlight. Ripe, complex flavors of melon and apple. Medium bodied and lively with a long finish hinting at minerality. Umm, great white.

When I finished it was only around ten. Still early for South Beach nightlife. The club next to the restaurant was just getting going. I was only halfway in the mood for some clubbing, still thinking about what I did or did not learn earlier. I went into the club propelled as if a slow current carried me along. It was just easy to follow the flow. The club design was contemporary, seating areas with low slung leather individual chairs and both loveseat and sofa size pieces. The leather came in multiple, muted colors. Some modernistic touches. Nice colors and forms on the walls. Some artwork where there were walls that had enough space. Primarily works of geometric figures in muted grays, oranges and browns. Had the feel of a high class and modern LA penthouse.

I picked a glass of wine that would follow the dinner nicely, complementing, not competing. As the bartender handed it over, I noticed a nice looking lady with penetrating dark eyes just to my right. We enacted one of many possible meeting rituals and soon were dancing. Her shimmery copper top swayed invitingly with the beat, its off the shoulder design highlighting her fabulous caramel skin. The club was gaining steam and patrons, and the energy level was rising. The beat here was Latin, salsa and rhumba and cha cha. I know them all and enjoy my limited chances to regain the moves. Domenica was a better dancer than I, but I was able to maintain the lead. Her hip movements were perfect, slinky and seductive. For Latin dances, getting those hips moving in rhythm and the accompanying leg motion dictate whether you look good and smooth or whether it shows you are just going through the paces. I'm not as good at that as I'd like to be. For Latin males, those hip movements seem to come more naturally than they do for me, but it doesn't matter so much because watching her hips move is where the heat is, and the heat was rising. We took a break from the floor. We decided a good Cognac would go well and enjoyed watching other dancers while we sipped until we were ready to dance again. We did. One more rhumba. Then we were out the door.

SEVEN

THE NEXT DAY I called Mrs. Reeves. Did Mr. Reeves take other people out sailing?

"Well, no, no, I don't think so." Pause.

"Oh, well, wait, maybe once in a long while, but rarely." Pause again.

"I think the last time I can remember anything like that was some time ago. He took a fellow from a company he was talking to, talking about whether there might be some mutual business opportunity. But, like I said, that was some time back."

"Do you remember a name?'

"Well, no, no, not right away."

"Anything about it, any mention?"

"Do you know if any business came of it?"

"Well, no, I don't think any did."

"It would help a lot if you were to come up with that business name."

"Well of course, I'll try."

An hour later she phoned me. She didn't find anything, but in the course of looking a name had tumbled the works of her mind, and she was sure that the business he had been talking to was Floridan Capital Partners.

I punched it up in my hotel's business center. Whattaya know. I had to accept that this was a deliberate name, setting itself apart from the thousands of Floridians. The business was on file with the state. The registered representative was listed as a law firm. That's a typical way to avoid naming any of the actual principals. There was a listing and an address.

I took a drive.

Following my information, it didn't take long to center in on the area. It was an in-between area, sometimes called an area of transition. I had passed through some areas that were just housing. Nice enough, not large houses, smaller individual lots, the occasional grouping of attached-type residential units. Then there were a couple of groupings of retail stores. Not strip center type, but a grouping of maybe five or six retailers, anchored by a drug store, then a fabrics shop, and linens/housewares, a hair/beauty salon, those kinds of uses. Then there would be a freestanding restaurant. Scattered among these were some one to three-story office building groups. This area wasn't a dedicated business park area nor retail mecca, it was an area that provided numerous services to nearby residents, from places to shop to places to work to places to eat. It had a more suburban, mixed use feel.

I found the address. It was a three-story brick building. Nice enough. Not remarkable. Not Class A.

I walked to the entry. The tenant listing was full. Most appeared to be small businesses. Insurance. Business consulting. Medical records management. More, similar.

Floridan Capital Partners was listed. Top floor. No other companies were listed as being on the third floor. Everyone else was either one or two. The whole top floor. Following the listing it said, 'Appointments by appointment only'. Was that supposed to be clever? Or a veiled warning.

I began a casual walk down the first-floor corridor, looking at office entry doors, signs, getting a feeling about the tenants and the building. The inner office doors all looked the same. The business name listings beside the doors were individualized. I walked back toward the elevator. I punched the button for the elevator. It came, the doors opened, I stepped inside. The control panel listed all three floors. I went to the second floor. I did the same thing on the second floor as I had on the first, walking casually down the hall, looking at doors, company nameplates, whether any information was presented. The offices gave the same impression as the outside had. A decent place for businesses to office, not a lot more, but not less either. I found myself back at the elevator. I found myself looking at the blank, closed doors. It would have been simple if there were multiple businesses on the third floor. Easy to walk down the hall, look around, see how things looked. But…

I thought about it for a minute. I'm probably not different from most people in this regard. If I have a good plan, I've got the confidence to barge ahead. But, like right now, when I wasn't quite sure how to represent my interest…so, I didn't feel quite so confident. What would I say—Hi, anyone here see a Mr. Reeves, you know, the guy you've gone sailing with? Oh, by the way, he's missing, know anything? That approach could get you a lot of stares, which I could deal with. But, it also might get a somewhat more aggressive reaction, and thinking about the menu of choices possible with this group, well...

I hit the up button on the call panel, stepped in when it came. As the elevator began to rise, I began conjuring a story.

'Uh, oh, I guess I wasn't paying attention, I thought I was going down...'

The elevator doors opened. Well, here we go. None but the brave, I hoped to myself. But my mind quickly followed up with or the crazy or the nuts. Come on, focus, and float with it. Calm. Yeah, right. I stepped out with my brain and heart racing each other, and ... I was in a hallway. There was a set of doors facing me. I had been guessing, with it being the only listing for the floor that I would come out of the elevator right into the office's reception area. Ahhhh! I had prepared myself, prepared being loosely interpreted, to plunge into the situation, work it out, dance if needed, figure my way in or out, on the move, as it were. But this was a stall. My 'not paying attention' line would have been lame maybe, but didn't work nearly so well to explain deliberately walking into the wrong office. I jumped as the elevator dinged—I was standing in the opening and the sensors wanted to know why. I stepped out.

I crossed the wide, carpeted hall.

On a wall plaque beside the doors, it said Floridan Capital Partners. Nothing else

Put my hand on the ornate door handle that I hoped operated one of the twin doors I faced.

Turned the door handle.

Opened the door.

Stepped inside.

The area I entered was fairly large and open. There were several large clubroom-like leather guest chairs separated by low tables with brass table lamps. Nautical themed pictures, ocean and ships depicted, were on several walls. Plush, textured designer carpet on the floor. The room felt luxury oriented.

There was not a receptionist, but there was a woman in sight working at a large desk. She looked up at me, with an expectant, 'Yes, if you're here you should know why' look. I wished I did.

I crossed the distance between us. She remained where she was. Her eyes never looked away, just focused on me with that slight raise of the eyebrows, the one that said, 'Yes, what do you want' without a spoken word. She was nice looking, older, but nicely cared for. The clothes were comfortable, casual workplace. I stopped in front of her and adopted my young businessman about to conquer the world look. She kept looking right at me.

"Hi, I'm Bob, with The Sunshine Local—the local weekly newspaper. Have you seen our paper?"

"No," she said, in that slightly drawn out 'no' we use when we mean 'No, I haven't seen it, and I'm not yet convinced I should care'.

"Well, we know that, being new, it will take awhile before everyone gets with us, but that's part of what we're doing, uh, what I'm doing, is going around to the businesses in our area to help see that they get acquainted with us, and so see what issues there are that concern them, so we can do our job of bringing information to our readers."

I paused just enough to then keep going and not allow her an opening to question me.

"So what business exactly goes on here at Floridan Capital Partners ?" Half a second pause. "And what issues do you see that deserve attention?"

"This is a private business...," she got out before I jumped back in.

"Oh, of course, and I don't mean to bother you, but if we don't get out and be involved, well, we may not do our best to serve the community."

"So what do you do here?"

"Uh, the partners manage some different business interests." She stopped, even against my encouraging, 'Yes, tell me, tell me' look.

"We just want to be good neighbors and contribute to everyone's best interests," I jumped back in.

"So, what areas are you in?"

"We manage...um, now look..."

I had her a little bit. The local paper, just trying to help, the earnestness I stuffed into the delivery.

It was beginning to be clear that there wasn't an easy, pat, 'we're accountants' or 'we're an advertising agency' answer to the 'what business?' question. I could only hold her off so long, and she jumped in.

"I'm sorry, the business interests here are varied, so it's

hard to classify us. We don't use advertising, so we probably don't fit your needs."

I hadn't said anything about advertising, hadn't asked them to place an ad, hadn't asked for a subscription. I guess she just grabbed onto the first excuse that came to her.

I was alternately holding her gaze, then looking away so as not to look at her too intensely, and stealing short, furtive glances around the office trying to spot a nameplate or any identifying thing at all. No luck with that.

"How about issues in the neighborhood?" I tried, "Like parking, or crime?" The annoying salesman tack, just keep trying to get your target interested.

Her eyes narrowed at me a little. Her look intensified.

She had been doing okay, putting up with this pest, but, it appeared that the look of intelligence she projected might be justified and was backed up by a working brain.

I decided I wasn't going to get much here, so discretion being the better part of valor, I started the wind down with the 'aw, shucks', eyes to the floor drop, then said, "Oh well, we don't want to turn a future friend into someone unhappy, so I'll just be going along then."

Her intense look softened only just a little by adding the beginning of a quizzical look that altered the set of her cheeks a bit. But she didn't say anything, which usually meant she hadn't bought it yet but wasn't ready to fire at me either.

I turned, walked my best not hurried but not jaunty walk away from her toward the doors, and when I got there, I couldn't help turning three-quarters and saying, 'thanks, bye'. Then I was out the door, across the hall and jabbing the elevator down button almost in one motion.

EIGHT

AT 7:30 THE NEXT MORNING, I was back at the building. I had coffee and fruit, and, best of all, a nice pastry from my hotel's selection. Neither coffee nor pastry without the other is quite as good as in combination, although sometimes I just have to settle for the coffee. I parked on the street. It was an easy place to see both entrances from the street to the building's surface parking area. It wasn't a huge area, and these parking entrances weren't far apart. I could also see the entrance to an underground parking area from where I watched.

It is much easier now to do an electronic search and come up with names, addresses, phone numbers, and more. But if you don't know a full name, whittling down the list can take time. I knew from past experience that just having the name wouldn't necessarily lead to much. And these particular names, too many people with the same names in this city. If I found an address that was in proximity, that might lead somewhere. Might not. I looked them up anyway. The result was maybe. Could be. Seventy-one listings for Mr. Hand.

Seventy-three listings for Mr. Barton. One hundred fifty listings for Mr. Cardenas. In this case, staking out residences to see where the occupant would go would be very time consuming. Since I thought I knew a location that these guys might go to, that seemed the better way to start. Staking out this place might narrow the list, and perhaps sort it out completely.

Sip some coffee, nibble some pastry. Not bad. But, I knew it would soon get tiring, the watching and the waiting. This is a hard part of this. Looking for something that you don't know what it is. Hoping that something will occur that will have meaning. Tiring, just waiting. So far, not many cars had already arrived and parked in the surface lot. As I watched, smaller vehicles were more abundant, with lots of young women exiting and walking into the building. I wanted to watch, to put in the time watching the parking lot, to make sure I had covered it. But, it was almost a no bet that the guys on the top floor would be destined for the underground garage. I watched. I sipped. Nibbled. Waited.

It was after 10:00 when the first likely candidate turned in off the street and down the ramp entrance to the underground garage. Black Mercedes. He had to slow to almost a stop at the garage entry as the ramp leveled from the slope. The few cars that had preceded this one, and that I didn't think to be likely possibilities because of the type, had already perfected my practice of spotting the license plate numbers on the slowing cars. I had noted the previous ones but this one I recorded with much more interest. By 11:00, six more likely higher-end vehicles had made my list. I hadn't hoped for it to be easy, hadn't hoped for Floridan Capital Partners, or Mr.

Hand, or 'follow me' to be stenciled on the side of the cars I wanted to identify and cut from the herd, but, it would have been nice. Oh well.

By this time I needed a break, so I just walked into the building. Easy.

Next, I found the door to the building stairwell. I thought I'd go to the underground parking area, look around, see what might be seen. The door was locked from this side. So, either no one on the first floor was allowed to park in this parking area, or, they had to access the parking by the elevator. Maybe no one but the third floor parked there. That would make it dicier if I were there looking around, and everyone who parked there knew everyone else. Hmmm. I went into the elevator anyway and went down.

The underground parking area was not large. Space for maybe two-dozen cars. There were fifteen here now. It was lighted with industrial type fixtures overhead. Low light, but not dark. I spotted the first of my likely cars, checked that I had the license plate number right, peered into the car interior to see if something helpful could be spotted. I found each of the likely suspects on my list. I found the black Mercedes last. I was looking into the interior of the car when I heard the elevator doors open. I dropped down alongside the car. A man exited the elevator and began walking my way. So, I didn't have the option of pretending I had just parked, crouched low here alongside the car. I could pretend I was checking the tire pressure, I suppose. The footsteps continued coming my way, then a beep went off that sounded practically on top of me. I knew it was the beep of a door being unlocked, and then a car door opened, then shuffle, shuffle, car door closed, then the clack and scratch of footsteps on the concrete floor resumed. Finally, another car door opened, shut, and a car started. The guy must have gone to the passenger door first of the car just one away, right beside the one I was crouched beside. When he finally got in and then drove off, I breathed out a long exhale.

It was harder to see in the back windows of the Mercedes, darker tint. The look through the front windows was clearer, but didn't offer more. I strode to the elevator, hoping no one would be trying to get off as I was trying to get on, then rode to the first floor, walked out of the building, and felt great when I walked into the warm sunny air.

I decided nothing was going to happen until later, so I got in my car and started to take a drive. I just started driving. Leisurely. Well, that is to say, as leisurely as possible with the combination of drivers Miami has on offer, from young hard-charging speed-is-all-consuming drivers, to, shall we say, drivers with more years of experience, who prize safety, and a dedication to their occupied space on the roadway, far more than speed, or even quickness. I managed my way among them, actually enjoying seeing the rush of a car to my left, followed by the full-on blaze of its taillights as the rusher encountered the not-to-be-rushed. This drive wasn't a search for anything specific, just a way to ease through some time. If something interesting or even just enjoyable encountered my eye and my mind, so much the better.

I made a turn here and a turn there, without finding much beyond merely pedestrian to entertain my senses. I made another turn and after just a short transit saw that the way ahead offered a promise of more interest. It was as if the road ahead narrowed just a little and at the same time, the landscaping at the sides of the road reached in on it creating a sense of entering a different realm. I went that way. The next distance did feel different. I drove slowly and let the charming characteristics of the area take me over and be my accompaniment. There was a sense of the lawns and houses whispering to me, 'ooh, look at what I have to show you', 'look here', 'look there', 'ooh, look at me'.

This was an older realm. Some of the properties had sumptuous green lawns of southern grasses beckoning toward the presentation of the home beyond. Bright and fragrant flowers emerged from their rooted bed to nod and wink as the slight breeze gave them animation. I encountered rugged but handsome stone steps winding upward, leading the eye and any visitor fortunate enough to be invited, up, away from the road and toward the shelter of mature trees overarching an entranceway. There were lawns manicured like an exclusive golf course and still others that leaned to a less controlled but equally pleasing presentation. There were properties that openly offered their visage to the road, while others allowed you to venture no farther from the road than the large, thick hedges that blocked the view beyond, providing privacy for the façade and for those on the other side of those hedges. In evidence were fountains, with water spilling freely over rims until captured finally at the base. There were walls, mostly low, made of stone, and made of brick, holding back islands of growing things and containing large blocks of verdant bushes that offered forth cascades of flowering blossoms that made it appear that the colored petals were floating on solid green waterfalls.

There was the occasional hint of sybarite life from briefly seen twinkles of filled swimming pools. Widely set in and among this pastoral expanse, when not obscured by their guardian hedges, were houses of stone and houses of stucco. Some rose impressively on their plot with high narrow windows topped with arches of glass peering down and obviously approving of their surroundings. Some homes spread wide and low, some tipping their long linear hats to Frank Lloyd Wright, while others signaled their appreciation to their Hispanic ranch heritage, hugging their earthen perch as intended. Each piece made its own contribution to this physical embodiment of art on a living grand scale. Driving through the neighborhood was like being in the artwork, having the chance to momentarily inhabit its nature and beauty.

I imagined the types of artwork contained in the spaces beyond the visible. In a low-slung hacienda there could be modern and contemporary explosions of color. In a strong, upstanding Tuscan façade there could be dangling mobiles moving gently to unseen forces hastening through lofty ceilings. One could imagine further that some of these spaces would incorporate highly detailed finishing touches, with carved wood moldings helping to frame arches over doorways and the perpendicular meetings of wall and ceiling overhead. Worked stone details would highlight intricate friezes on fireplace faces. These spaces also seemed inclined to exhibit well-done interiors, with artwork to complement.

I pictured the lives that were being lived within these walls, within these rooms.

My imagination took over. Something I've enjoyed in many parts of the world has been visiting museums and historic abodes that open their doors to the public, giving a glimpse of the trappings that once upon a time framed the dwelling portion of the existence of the inhabitants.

I thought of visiting chateaus in France, castles and palatial estates across Europe. I thought of grand American examples such as the Newport mansions. The walls and ceilings and floors and adornments of these habitats contributed to how those residents saw themselves and colored their relationships with the other inhabitants of that time and their world.

While I'm always looking at paintings, many museums have displays featuring historic room furnishings and decoration. I enjoy standing inside these examples and letting the space inhabit me. I wonder if previous inhabitants admired the artistry of their space, or whether they simply moved through it accepting it as their due.

My mind continued down this path, thinking about Greek and Roman and other ancient civilizations' contributions to how we live today, to our homes and our arts. At about this time I realized that the neighborhood was changing, that the realm formed by creative hands and natural beauty that I had been traversing was becoming more ordinary. The spell was, for now, broken. It was time to turn back to the work that faced me. But I will be able to resummon the interest and awe that had occupied me for a while, and I was very appreciative.

I made a turn and bid adieu to this lovely neighborhood, this lovely realm that had occupied and enchanted my mind for this bit of time. Visiting interesting places and losing yourself in them engages the mind's creativity. It's a very good thing to do. It's a part of the artistic tradition, observing, both physically and mentally, the details of someone else's expression of artistic display, even if it is a very different expression or a different form than your own pursuit. This exposes you to other ways and means of conveying the creative spirit that is central to artistic expression. It must be practiced.

NINE

AT THREE O'CLOCK, I was back parked in position by the building. Just as I had figured my guys to be later arrivers at work, I figured they would also be early departers. At 3:35, a gold Lexus that was on my list pulled out of the parking garage. As he slowed to make his first turn a half-block away, I slid out into the street and began to follow. Everyone I know has seen enough detective shows or read enough books to think they know how it works. Can't start off right behind, too noticeable. Can't do odd attention-grabbing things. Most people do notice, to very varying degrees, the vehicles that are accompanying them in their limited travel sphere—right in front, to the front side, right behind. But when traveling on main trafficways, people don't get alerted typically, mostly just semi-consciously noting—hmmm, going the way I'm going. So, it was easy at first to follow. The person following is certainly at a higher state of readiness—looking to see if lights will change uncooperatively, looking to see if other cars will pull in and increase the comfortable gap to an uncomfortable one, or adjusting if all your buffer cars pull out leaving you right behind, making you feel like you want to be dragging your feet or backpedaling, or wondering whether you should be looking sideways out the window or appearing to be working very hard on changing your radio stations. It's best to do what you can, maintain that heightened alertness, sometimes drive aggressively to maintain position, sometimes be very easy going. He made it easy, with his pathway that was in the main traffic flow.

I employed the method, following the Lexus not too close, trying to be not too far. At one light, yellow far enough in advance to assure that anyone not stopping would go through on red, ah gee, he did it. A plague on red-light runners. For the next two lights, I scanned the road ahead to try to spot an exit or to reacquire the target. After another and larger intersection, a number of the people, going my way, decided home was elsewhere, and the cars thinned out. Ahead were two similar-looking gold cars. Well, maybe those are good enough odds. Gold car two slowed, and then pulled into a high-rise condo, of which we were entering a forest of. It was not my guy. I pressed it a little to get closer to the other golden, but soon he executed the same maneuver as the first and entered into a high-rise complex, and when I got close enough to the complex, knew he had entered its parking structure. And this one was my gold. So, I had an address, 1120 Seaway Boulevard. When I checked the address against the names I was targeting, there it was, Robert Barton, 1120 Seaway Blvd, Unit 1502. I had one of them. The condo unit was a possible hiding place for my disappeared man if it was of his own volition, but if it wasn't, this would not be the most likely. I could manage getting into a building like this, but then what? Sitting around the lobby was likely to be not too productive, besides boring. Better information would be gotten elsewhere. Still, I have one of them.

TEN

THE NEXT MORNING I was back at the building again. Now that I knew one of the players, perhaps the others might keep the same hours, and arrive around the same time. Maybe not. But, I looked, kept track of who did arrive, paying particular attention to my target list, but willing to add any new possibilities. In fact, the black Mercedes and the gold Lexus did arrive within about ten minutes of each other. But I didn't have anything yet on the Mercedes, and a third partner was not yet willing to be easily smoked out. I decided to venture another excursion into the parking garage. The first time in I had noted license plates, etc., and I had also noted relative parking positions. There were no obvious signs that parking spaces were assigned, but I thought that if the cars were in the same places, it might tell me something. So into the building I went, checked the stair door just to see, it was still locked, and down in the elevator. The two cars I had identified were close to where they were before, but not exactly. Three of the cars on my list were exactly where they had been, but they were also the earliest arrivers of the bunch. The others were located in no pattern that was discernible to me. I took the stairway up, and exited without incident. My plan was to return to the building at an anticipated departure time for these vehicles, and follow a second car, so I had some time to kill, again. The nature of the beast.

There are wonderful art galleries throughout Miami, and I had a few favorites, so that was my plan, go enjoy. I consider myself a contemporary artist, but that means many and varied things to people in general, and even to other artists and patrons themselves. Colors, structure of those colors, and an attempt to create what, for lack of twenty textbook paragraphs might most easily be described as movement, were what motivated me most. Most people think they grasp the element of color, since most everyone thinks they see the blue sky, green grass and red and yellow butterflies, or other equally identifiable objects or creatures. Color is much more complex of course, but people know- what colors they like and what colors they don't. Structuring the colors is less known to people in general. How they relate, what emotions or response can be generated by certain colors adjacent or in proximity to others. How about the size and shape of the color blocks, or dashes, or drops? How about their placement at different points on a canvas?

A common tenant of English landscape painting was and is to draw your eye in from the bottom of the canvas, along a road created to do that, or a stream, or along any number of compositional elements to accomplish the purpose. Then they want to deposit you on the horizon, and see if you'll look left, or right, or up, or back down. The skill in directing that movement of your eye through the piece contributes mightily to the eventual acclaim that that piece is likely to receive. The same can be true with expressionism, or abstraction. One goal is to direct your attention, in the way chosen by the artist, to see colors in a pathway of that artist's design, or colors and shapes, or juxtaposition of shapes, or shapes and color, trying to create a reaction in the viewer, or trying to communicate the point of view, or emotions, or thoughts of the artist. The ways of doing this are infinite, but the skill with which it is accomplished divides the few from the many.

Great, and good, artists I've known are always looking, always trying or evaluating, another way of expressing what it is they wish to convey when they create. Lifelong learning is good for everyone in every pursuit, of course, but for an artist, it is a requirement. For this, and other reasons, I like to look at galleries that feature all kinds of artistic works. I like to go look at abstractions, and try to see both what I see and what the artist might be trying to have me see. It is not science, however, so see what you want. I particularly like to visit galleries exhibiting two different presentations or artistic styles, and then see if there are comparisons or contrasts. I am also influenced by the exteriors of galleries or museums. I love galleries with the façade of old English or French bookstores, with tall, narrow windows above paneled bases, looking like fine cabinetry. Or very weathered cabinetry. That exterior look is just appealing to me. It doesn't say anything about the quality of the art in the gallery, but it does draw me in on that first impression of the outside. Another favorite building style is sleek modernism, with large uniform windows, often accented in steel surrounds, horizontal and vertical linework, and the monumental impression they exude as they command the space they occupy. I made my way to one of each and spent the next several hours happily looking, thinking, drinking in different realizations of artistic conception.

At the anticipated time of departure of my persons of interest, I was back at the building. I had planned to go once again to the parking garage, so that I wasn't just sitting and waiting for an already departed vehicle, but I had hardly stopped the car when the gold Lexus exited, so I sat and watched. Before he was out of sight, the black Mercedes emerged. Better to be lucky than…

I employed the method, following the Mercedes. With this driver, the main roads again were the pathway, making being spotted less likely, but allowing the vagaries of number of drivers and light changes to make the task more difficult. Traffic was much heavier going the way we were going. At one light I was right where I wanted to be, we were both in the second lane. The lane next to us, the curb lane, was also full of cars, and one delivery truck. When I saw the driver of the truck get out of the cab I knew there would be trouble. The red light turned, cars started to move, cars behind the truck hit their horns and their turn signal simultaneously. Some of the curb lane cars were let in, others just poked their noses out and with additional honking, vacated the stalled lane. Mercedes made it through easily. I did not. For the next two lights, I scanned the road ahead to try to reacquire the target in the bumper-to-bumper congestion. I kept going, you never know what might occur. I didn't regain sight of the right black car. I wanted to be mad, but there really was no point to it. I felt urgency though, another day gone by and not much to show for it. I didn't even know if the car would have led me anywhere.

ELEVEN

IT WAS NECESSARY to return to the building the next day. My gold Lexus driver was Mr. Barton. I had one of the names I had been given at the yacht club attached to car and address, so I knew that, but it was far from enough. I might need a different plan. A similar progression of cars entered the parking garage, including black and gold. No actionable thing happened to make me feel I could identify the third.

Today I wasn't sure how I wanted to proceed. Visiting the galleries had been enjoyable yesterday. What to do today if there was a time lapse? Visiting the galleries benefitted my mind, but action on this matter was becoming paramount. I sat and thought about it. Indecision. Really don't like it. But in these kinds of pursuits, more frequently than not, I had to adjust, summon patience, think what might unfold, see if any of my musings about the facets of the case could be fashioned into a gem. Small measures of preparation helped. Because I felt uncertain, I brought coffee along this morning. Luck favors the prepared. So I sipped some, and perused a newspaper.

After awhile I stretched, yawned, and tried to focus my mind on a particular pursuit that would contribute to knowledge. Nothing bubbled to the surface and I started to feel a bit of restlessness combined with annoyance. It wasn't going to be too long before it would be noon. I hadn't been here observing the comings and goings during the noon hour yet.

I decided to sit and wait. It felt like a choice, although it might have just been a way to gain some time to come up with a real plan.

Patience. I've become practiced at it, but it is not particularly satisfying.

At about 11:45 the black Mercedes emerged from the parking garage, single occupant. I turned on my car, almost reflexively, because my mind had not concluded what I was going to do. The next thing that happened made it a no brainer. The gold Lexus pulled out next. I followed. It was easy. Black took the lead, gold seemed content to follow. If black made it through a light, but gold didn't, there didn't seem to be a concern. The parade rolled on. I began to conclude they knew their destination and it would be the same. It was only about fifteen minutes into the parade before black turned into a restaurant parking lot and parked. Gold followed black into the entrance from the street and down the small driving lane of the lot and found a place a few spaces away. I continued on the street a half block farther along and turned down a side street bordering the restaurant's lot. There was an entrance to the lot off this side street and I pulled in and drove along the driving lane further away from the restaurant building than the one black and gold had pulled into.

I parked two rows of spaces away from black and gold with a small compact car in front of me. The roof of the compact car was low enough that I could track them, with good views of them between other parked cars. Neither of them exited their cars immediately, maybe completing calls, or who knows what. The driver door of a third car, parked closest to the restaurant entrance than the others, opened. The driver got out, walked to within about ten feet of the entrance, stopped, looked back into the parking area, and I thought he was looking at me. His gaze was not to my distance however, just to that first row of parked cars. Both the black and the gold drivers got out, walked toward the entrance, and joined the waiting guy. No handshakes, no pause, no hey, how ya doin?, they just all walked into the restaurant together. I watched, waited. I looked at the restaurant to see if I could spot where they might be seated, but there weren't that many glass surfaces anyway, so I felt parking lot activity was not generally going to be evident to those inside. I waited a little longer, then got out and approached car three. It was a cream-colored Audi. I noted the license plate number. I was just about convinced that the black Mercedes was in on it. Was this Audi car driver number three? Very possibly.

The area we were in had the look of fairly typical older Miami streetscapes. Single story buildings mixed with two stories. Storefronts proclaiming their wares in English and Spanish. Lots of small, probably family run, restaurants, blazoned with the different words that mean things to eat. COMIDA, CAFECITO, and, BAKERY

The cultural diversity adds to the spirit of adventure I sense when I think about all these people taking on the risks and rewards of running their businesses and finding ways to meet the needs of the neighborhood population.

Law firms offering assistance with drivers licenses.

Income tax shops promising Maximum Devolcion.

Shops offering a multitude of services: loans, notary, document assistance, check cashing.

Offerings of GUAYABERAS.

Offerings of CUBAN COFFEE, with Authentic Cuban Flavor.

Many shops titled PELUQUERIA, ESTILISTA, et BARBERO.

I'm not sure of the differences except I do go to a barber and I don't go to beauty shops.

Single-purpose shops offering flowers, or liquor.

Not surprisingly though, many offer several services within their walls: Pawn and Jewelry; Liquor and Check Cashing.

And, of course, many outlets offering CIGARS.

Contributing to the sense of place that makes street blocks like this feel more like a small town business area than just a drab office block is that more than not of these business storefronts have colorful paintings of bright flowers and other flora decorating their fronts softening the commercial feel, making the entire street section welcoming.

I spotted a Comida proclaiming Cuban Sandwiches. I stopped. The shop looked clean and already had quite a few customers. Okay, I'll try.

I went back to the restaurant. It was just as I had left it. I found a place to park on the adjacent side street where I could see the restaurant entrance just enough. I was also parked so I could leave the curb and head directly onto the main street accessing the restaurant. I unwrapped the Cubano and dug in. Good initial mouth flavor. Um. It had been done right. I savored it slowly. Really good. Great to find a small shop that did it right. Not quite Versailles or Columbia, but very good.

It wasn't a long lunch. The three of them emerged and walked in the direction toward the parked cars. The driver went to his black Mercedes and the newest guy got in the passenger side. Gold went to his car. I had already chosen to follow black. Two for one, of course. Black pulled from his space, and gold dropped in behind. Were they going to make it easy again or split up in traffic? For the first turn onto the main street they stayed together. I would have to stay behind gold, and if they weren't going to the same place that could make it difficult to stay with black when they went their separate ways. They didn't. It was easy again for awhile, but eventually, black pulled from the relative safety of the main trafficway and started into a less trafficked, more industrial part. Our parade here would be more noticeable.

The industrial area was laid out in a grid. We were traveling along a long section of the grid, and I could see to my sides that the intersecting streets were much shorter sections. The black car looked to be continuing on a straight path, for now, so I took the next left, abandoning my caboose position. When I got past the short section of the grid, I turned right and was on a parallel street. This was a warehouse/industrial area, with little activity on the street. I hit it. Hard. In three long grid street sections I didn't mow anyone down, didn't hit a drainage pan section in the street that would've sent me flying almost like Steve McQueen's Bullitt in San Francisco, even though this street was flat, but I also hadn't caught a glance of the gold car parallel to me. I turboed it for two more long sides of the gridded blocks, then spun it right and back to the parallel street. Probably because of the adrenaline rush from the speed I turned left onto the parallel street, without regard, really, for what might be there. I thought I might be right behind gold. Maybe I'd be between them. I deflated fast when there was neither in sight.

I drove fast to the next intersection, looked left then right, nothing. Hit it again to the next intersection. This time I looked right first and just caught the gold as it disappeared onto a parallel street several blocks on this grid that was starting to make me feel like I was a game piece in an old video game. I shot ahead to gold's last turning and again saw nothing. But this time I felt better about it. The air close to the ocean contains a magic. There is the scent of water in the air, a perfume that combines moisture with salt, and some other ingredient that I've never completely identified, something organic, maybe dissolving seaweed. There is also something baitfish like. Briny. Whatever the composition, it is an elixir, at once recognizable and instantly uplifting. I had sensed this presence a bit further back, but with the chase in progress had postponed enjoying it. The air conditioning in the car delays the reception, but the elixir scent infiltrates. I rolled the window down and took in a welcome gulp of it. I was calm about losing sight of them and was appreciating the smell, and taste, of that gulp of air. Part of my appreciation, beyond the sensual, was because it also meant there was a limit to how far away my prey could get. I felt I would be able to close in on them. The sea is an indomitable barrier to mere automobiles.

I started a search, making sure I knew my starting spot. I drove the grid, up and back. At the far reach of my grid search, the ocean, more likely the seaway, would come into view. This was the highpoint of the path, up, down, reach the apogee of the grid search, get a quick view of water, start back away from the water again. It took about twenty passes, but then there they were. In plain sight. The black and the gold. They were parked inside a fenced yard that was part of a small warehouse—appearing single-story structure. I couldn't see it at this point, but a dock area was probably part of the complex. I had seen many at the water barrier highpoints of the grid search. There was no particular identifying mark or anything on the warehouse. No sign, no company name like Universal Exports, nothing. A number identification was on the side of the building, maybe a street address, although I hadn't seen any street signs in quite awhile. Maybe the whole area had one street identification, then you had to know the progression of numbers to find where you were going. Or maybe everyone who came here already knew exactly where they were going and which spot was theirs. Current fire department rules wouldn't allow for this sort of lackadaisical approach, too hard for emergency services to know where to go. But this area was old and had been here a long time. Maybe if something happened here where help might seem needed, nobody summoned it, just dealt with it themselves. I stopped short of their parked cars, trying to spot a place that would let me observe unobtrusively.

A half block further in I found a place more ramshackle than the rest. It was a building that looked unoccupied and the surrounding parking or yard area definitely was unoccupied. It looked like there might have been a fire in part of the building as well. See, they either didn't call, or the fire department couldn't find it. But the lack of any noticeable enterprise around it made it good for watching, and if anyone approached me, it would be easy to play the "looking for a spot to rent, heard this might be available" card. The yard area here was not fenced in front, so it was convenient to pull in and stop. I couldn't see a lot of what might be going on where black and gold were, but most of what might be going on wasn't seeable from the street even if I had been parked right in front of it. I would have to wait and watch until they moved, or until someone noticed me and shooed me away. I did this for awhile. But there comes a feeling of sitting too long in one spot, of being out in the open, of being exposed. When I started feeling this way, I drove off slowly, making notes on the most direct path back with notations of any landmarks that seemed fixed and unlikely to alter. I knew I would be back under cover of darkness.

TWELVE

 softly when I drove past the industrial-looking building that I had found with the help of black and gold. The area had just the slightest bit of light from two low rent light fixtures attached to the wall near the entrance door. There didn't seem to be any activity. The black and gold cars were gone. The closest adjacent building and facilities appeared to be in the same state of retirement from the activities of the day, ready to rest wearily until a new day brought the denizens of their haunts back. I drove past for a few long grid length blocks, turned, drove three short lengths, then turned parallel again to the street where the building sat, and drove past the location on that parallel but once-removed street. I had not found a better stopping point than the, hopefully, abandoned building and lot that had been my vantage point earlier, so that was where I wound my way back to, parked the car with it poised to run away to the extent possible while still keeping it somewhat secluded.

The fence surrounding the parking lot had a big, swing-it-open-yourself chain-link gate in it, which was closed and padlocked. The fence at this side of the yard went back toward where it would intersect with the water. I moved toward this intersection, because it was darkest there, and that was where I planned to scale the fence. Well, the fence didn't go all the way to anywhere, it just stopped, two feet short of a low wall that delineated the edge of the industrial spaces from the access to the docks. The low roofed industrial building in the lot adjacent to this one was about twenty feet removed and didn't contribute to securing the yard, so despite the fence, it wasn't a lock-down high-security setup. I scooted around the edge of the fence instead of climbing over it. Tough choice. As I moved into the yard continuing along the low wall, no spotlights came on, no sirens went off, at least none that I could hear.

As I moved along the low wall, the layout of the property became far more clear than what could be determined from the street. The actual building was smaller than it appeared. The wall that projected back toward the water wasn't part of the building although it was clad with the same material as the building. Instead, the wall formed an enclosure area behind the building, and this enclosure area had a partial roof that followed the roofline of the building, but covered only a portion of the area behind the building, allowing for a sheltered area that was used for storage. A tingling sense rushed through me. Adrenalin. Alertness. Readiness. I made my way toward what I could now discern as the rear of the building through this storage area portion. I went more slowly now because where I thought that the place was vacated for the day, I found that in the hidden rear yard there were two parked vehicles, both too new, clearly not just being stored, and indicating someone was on hand or had been around more recently than made me comfortable.

I reached the rear of the building. There were several large door openings where the doors were hinged and could swing back into the building, barn door style, to create openings large enough to accommodate a car or pickup. All were closed. There were two windows, boarded up from the inside, so they afforded no insight into the building. With my movement through the rear spaces of this area no lights had popped on, and still no sirens or other indication of surveillance had manifested, although that didn't mean that there weren't any. Maybe this was just a small business operation of some sort and had nothing to do with anything that would help me figure out what was going on. Worse, maybe nothing was going on, and I was snooping around in the dark on a fool's mission.

Suddenly two things happened in such rapid succession that they were almost simultaneous. Car tires sounded from the other side of the wall of the storage enclosure area and the sails of a boat appeared almost at the dock at the border of the sheltered rear yard. The boat moved soundlessly. There wasn't even the low slap sound of water against the hull. I was already moving with the tire sound, ducking low, moving along the enclosing wall of the storage area, and had nowhere to go except toward the portion of the storage area closer toward the water and away from the rear of the building. I was still moving when the car, without headlights, turned the corner of the storage area and pulled into the open rear yard area. The car was very dark. My mind was racing my feet. Straighten up and run for it. The thought flashed past. Okay, then duck. Hide. My brain and my feet chose hide. There was clutter, unimportant leftover stuff in this back corner of the covered storage area. Just twenty feet around the corner would be my run to daylight chance, but the car was already stopped and the opening click of car doors made its warning.

I shrank back into the boxes and leftover wood pieces. Two men emerged from the car and stood looking toward the dock. The dock was not visible to me, off to my left, hidden by the rear wall of my protective but limiting enclosure. The rest of the open rear yard and the rear of the building were visible though the scene was taking on a late evening tone. One of the men moved to the building and with soft clanks opened a set of doors and swung them inward. The opening gaped. He then walked back to the car and past it, toward the dock, following the path of his partner. It was only moments before men appeared walking from the dock toward the open doors carrying large bags that obviously contained some weight. Large duffel looking bags. They were large sail bags, packed with something much heavier than any normal sails. If there were sails in those bags they must have been made of canvas from the seeming bulk, and that's certainly not the current state of the sail maker's art. Even in the dark it was easy to tell that nobody looked like a casual sailor, nobody had on boat shoes, no white shorts, no polo shirt and blue blazer, not even a captain's hat. The men obviously knew their business. No lights came on. Very little sound was made. Men moved from left to right practically in front of me, coming from the dock and entering into the building's dark barn door opening, then back. This was a smart operation. Better this way, far less noticeable than on TV, where seven guys are standing around with automatic weapons. It was over in just a few minutes.

Someone pulled the doors shut and locked them with a soft click. The men got into all three parked vehicles. No interior lights came on. The first two parked vehicles drove quietly around my wall, the third pulled in a circle through the yard and followed the two out. My eyes had adjusted to the night as theirs had. The hood ornament on the last car was unmistakable.

I listened as the tires that had alerted me retreated. I listened for some clinking that would indicate the fence gate shutting. I hadn't heard such a sound before the tires arrived, and I didn't hear it now.

THIRTEEN

AFTER A WAIT, straining to hear or see something in the darkness, I emerged. Slowly. Cautiously. Peering into the darkness. Seeing darkness, and little else. I was in a place where I felt the objects around me provided background cover, where I blended in, where I was less exposed. My next move would have to be into the open, to turn the corner of the end wall of the storage area. Then there would be the twenty feet along the wall until the next corner. Would I be in the middle of that distance when someone stepped out from behind the corner to meet me? Heck, would someone be just around this first corner I was about to turn? I was pretty sure no one was left behind in the rear portion of the yard behind the building, but the appearance of the crew into previously vacant space had been snap fast. Would it, could it, happen again? More likely one or two, not the whole crew, but...

I paused beside the last object providing cover and looked into the darkness I could see and made ready for the darkness I could not. I edged my eyes around the corner first, using my low, bunched shadow position. Nothing for me to see. Now I moved quickly to the corner and looked around. There was more light toward the street portion of the building's front yard, and I could see the gate of the fenced-in front. It was closed. There were no vehicles in sight, but the front area could not be seen in its entirety from this vantage. I snapped my head back around to inspect from I had been. No movement. I really wanted to see what I could about the boat. No way to do it but to do it. Now. I stayed against the wall and moved back to my other corner. Again I looked around the corner, this time back into the rear yard. I moved sideways until I was against the low wall where it ended and the dock area began. The dock ended at a hoist. The hoist contributed to the look that this was a working boatyard. But it was hard to see the exact condition of the hoist. Maybe it was rusted, having hauled its last hull from the sea years ago.

Along the water were three slips for mooring. In the center slip was the sailboat. The crew had done their work. The boat was covered with a very dark, likely black, hull cover. I slowly and carefully moved toward the stern. The planking of the dock felt firm. There was very little give, and no squeaking to accompany the give. I eased up to the stern of the covered hull. No markings were visible. The cover came down over the gunwale and draped along the hull. My fingers felt along the edge of the cover. It was tightly attached. I worked my fingers just barely under the cover and strained to see if it would slide upward. I wanted to find a name or registration number if possible. While my fingers strained, my ears caught the sound of soft footfalls on the wooden planks of the dock.

Out of the darkness a man appeared, as if rising out of the dock itself. In the dark he didn't have focus on me yet. He was close enough to me for me to see the mean smile on his face. He spotted me. No longer trying to sneak, but suddenly too close, he swung the barrels of the shotgun into my side in an attempt to blow me in half at point-blank range.

Yeah, well, my reactions are good. I caught the barrels of the shotgun as he snapped it forward to level it on me and kept it moving past my body. Its thunder roared. The noise and force of the discharge stunned me, but didn't do what he had intended. Partly out of reaction, partly out of the fear/surprise rush, and partly out of the necessity of not permitting a second chance to blow a hole in me, even against the force of the kick, I was able to get a good hold on the shotgun. Now, likely due to his surprise at not accomplishing his maneuver, I was able to twist what I was holding onto. Snap. The shotgun came out of one of his hands and he stumbled sideways a couple steps with the momentum from jerking the gun out of his hand. I went with him on the sideways move and with my balance intact could give one more quick twist to the gun, moving my controlled momentum into his stumbling momentum, and down he went, releasing the last of his hold on the gun. Instantly I took off running.

I heard the first words that he spoke as he grunted and spat out 'Hey'. But my sprint was in full flight and I was off the dock, made the distance to the fence end and around, then around the adjacent building corner. I sprinted for the next corner, and around it. I sprinted into the darkness. I was still holding the shotgun.

I approached my car cautiously. I stayed in shadows and observed it for five minutes, maybe a little more. I certainly wouldn't wait for daylight, so it was time to go. I went to my car, opened it, got in, and shut the door only to the first click. My interior light did not come on either. I had learned, and begun to practice a long time ago, the no interior light. No signal to others, at least from this. Since it was a more or less permanent fix, explaining the no light setup to dates was also fun. But I'm not thinking about that now. Starting the car was another matter. Perhaps everyone in surveillance would eventually adopt cars and engines like some of the hybrids that make no sound when started. If you're used to the conventional engine burst, it takes a little getting used to with the hybrids to know if the car is even going to go when you press the accelerator. My headlights were switched to off. I started the car, drove away, didn't touch the brakes until I was around the corner. No tracer fire followed me.

On the drive away, while watching for any lights to follow me, or hood ornaments, I speculated about the enterprise. I supposed it could be a good cover, the sailboat. Quiet. Somewhat unobtrusive. Blending into the recreational activity in the area instead of criminal commercial activity. These guys were smart. The building, yard, and dock sure had the makings of a workable operations base. I wished there had been time to see if anything could be spotted inside the building. And then there was the night guard. There was no mistaking what he would have done if he could.

FOURTEEN

THE NEXT DAY found me starting off with coffee, fresh, marvelous, bursting in the mouth melon, and bacon, a guilty pleasure. I was in the process of concluding that it was time for some help. After the sipping and savoring, I headed out. The Miami police station is in a big modern building. I parked in the large public lot and made my way past landscaping islands of shell ginger, yaupon holly and wax myrtle inter-mixed with weigela and hydrangea, some blossoming with colorful flowers and the whole of the entourage exuding a soft fragrance carried abundantly through the moist morning air. The heat was only beginning to build, and the pleasantness of the landscaping in the parking lot belied the hard and often unpleasant work that went on inside the station itself. I entered, went through the security routine, and headed for the detectives.

I hadn't called because I didn't know anyone here and couldn't quite see starting the conversation I was hoping to have over the phone. So I was ready to just walk in and see what card fate would hand me. Might get someone who would think I was loony. Might get someone who I couldn't tell it all to because they might conclude I wasn't quite walking the straight and narrow myself last night. I hoped there would be another choice. I retain an image, from television and movies and from my own experiences many years ago, of guys like me walking into the detective den, with guys at desks sitting with their feet up on the desks talking gruffly into the phones, the ones with cords attaching them to the old desk sets. You pretty much can't just walk in on this vignette anymore, particularly in large cities.

My first encounter was with a reception desk setup, and perhaps this method helps sort out some of the things that are worth looking into from the mostly crazed visions that haunt some minds. In my opening statement of purpose I mixed in a missing person with possible drug smuggling activity. It must have sounded possible enough that it got me through the first gatekeeper. I was led to an open office space, it looked to be a place where a quiet but frank discussion could take place without intruding into the real office working space of the detective. I sat, and a fellow walked in through the open door. Young but not young/green looking. Young and yeah I've already been around the block a couple of times looking. He introduced himself with a pleasant manner, Detective Ramirez, a little formal, no first name given, 'you came to me after all', that's okay, then got to it, what can I help you with? I told him. The missing businessman. The connection to Floridan Capital Investors. Then the sailboat. Then the 'cargo' run and unloading in the dark. He listened, looked at me with briefly raised eyebrows a couple of times, but he let me keep going. No tsk, tsk. At times he made a little sideways twist of his head like you do when you've heard something you perhaps weren't expecting or found to be out of character with your expectations, but at the same time you're going, well, I guess it could happen that way.

He had been mostly quiet, only the briefest of questions or quick clarifications as we went along. Finally he said, "That's pretty interesting."

"So you think there's a connection between your disappeared businessman, and the connection might be the boat. And, the boat might be bringing in, well, who knows, drugs most likely, but there could be other explanations."

"Yes, that's the direction I think this is leading."

"Well, it's not far fetched."

"Most of the operations that we learn about use motorboats, with the notion that they can run if an intercept is attempted."

"Sometimes it's bigger boats, bulkier boats, to carry as much as possible with the greatest number of onboard hiding places as possible.

A sailboat might work. They would feign a pleasure sail if the coast guard or police boat patrols run into them."

This was going pretty well, I thought. But I also knew pretty soon he was going to ask me what I wanted him to do. I wasn't sure yet.

"Okay then, so you could be on to something we would be interested in. Pursuing it might help you find your missing person, or maybe not. It's not yet enough to go on for me to do much more than tell you thanks for making me aware of it and I'll keep it in mind. Unless you have a plan."

Here it comes, I thought to myself.

He had paused for a moment and looked at me expectantly.

When I didn't help, he came right out with it.

"Okay, you haven't said anything. What do you want me to do?"

"First, thanks for taking this so well, for listening to me. I don't know exactly what I want you to do. The fact that you haven't said, 'hey, we got guys like this around every corner' is appreciated."

He looked right at me and grinned.

"The best I could hope for is that if I stumble across more, that I can call you, you'll remember me, and maybe you'll act if I find enough."

"Yes," he said.

"Yes, I was pretty sure you were intending to keep on, stumbling about, as you put it, and there is enough of a good basis in your story, so yes. I'm going to give you the magic number, the one that gets through to me as directly as whatever situation I might be in will allow. But remember, it's not a bat signal. Don't get yourself in too deep and count on a rescue. You won't know if I'm chasing down a gang of my own or asleep. But it's the best I have."

He gave me the number.

"I'll only use it if I can make it worth your while, or that's what I'll try for."

"Good, but, if these guys are drug dealers, or smugglers or anything close, they're dangerous and don't forget it."

"Thanks."

"Uh, there's one more thing."

"I told you about my encounter with Mr. mean smile, and about him swinging the shotgun at me."

"Unh huh."

"Well, I ended up with shotgun."

He gave me an exaggerated raised eyebrows look that quickly morphed into his grin.

"Unh huh."

"It's downstairs in my car, in the parking lot."

He just looked to the ceiling, still with the grin, and said, 'Ha!'

We went down to my car, I opened the trunk, and he retrieved the shotgun carefully and placed it in an evidence bag he had brought along. They would get fingerprints from it. Mine. Mr. mean smile. Maybe they would match up the prints to someone they had something on. Maybe they wouldn't find a match, but if not, they would now have the prints and the shotgun, and maybe my shotgun assailant would show up again at some point in this adventure. Detective Ramirez thanked me, took the shotgun in the evidence bag and headed back toward the building, but turned after just a step or two and looked at me.

"Good luck on the rest of your stumbling about out there."

I smiled back at him.

"…and be careful out there" he grinned at me.

Now it was my turn to look skyward and laugh.

FIFTEEN

I SAT IN my car. I was happy about the way it had gone with Detective Ramirez. Detective Anton Ramirez. That was a little bit of a different first name, but, Miami, all of South Florida, it's just a great big melting pot. Sounds Swiss to me. Maybe his parents just made it short for Antonio. Don't know. But, I was glad to have his number. It would almost certainly be useful. But his caution rang true. These guys are crooks and will do what suits them. Making a call probably couldn't result in an instant summons and the cavalry riding to the rescue. Better consider that with whatever I did next.

During our discussion, I had given the detective the car, license plate and address information I had ascertained for gold car, Mr. Barton. I also gave him the black car and cream car and license numbers and told him I expected them to be connected to a Mr. Hand and a Mr. Cardenas. Before I left his office, he confirmed that I had ID'd numbers two and three. We checked the addresses. Another high-rise condo building for Contreras. The address for Mr.

Hand was the office building. No help there. Now on to what course?

What I decided should be next shouldn't involve any rescue by the cavalry. I started toward the yacht club. Pulling onto the grounds it felt again like an oasis of calm, and even a little relief from the heat was offered by all the landscaping. I followed practically the same path I had taken before toward the docks and the hut. The fellow I was looking for was just finishing helping two young couples as they cast off and headed out.

"Hi, Josh," I said. "Don't know if you remember me from a few days ago, talking about Mr. Reeves and his sailboat."

"Oh, yeah, sure, hi," he said.

"Well, I'm still working out a business deal with Mr. Reeves, but he's pretty busy and not always easy to pin down."

"He also invited me to go out for a sail with him. Apparently he likes to talk business on the boat, just like a lot of people like to do on the golf course."

Nothing I had said really required an answer yet from Josh, so he didn't say anything.

"We haven't been able to pin down a time for that sail yet, but I thought of something, a way to make it easier for us to hook up, and I wondered if I could get your help."

I still hadn't proposed any action directly to him, so I continued.

"Here's what I'm thinking, and you can tell me if it will be okay."

I pulled out a hundred dollar bill that I had folded and put in my pocket where I could easily, casually like, retrieve it.

I held the hundred dollar bill so that it could be seen, but wasn't yet being proffered.

"I would like to give you my phone number, and when Mr. Reeves takes the boat out, you could call me. That way I'd know both not to bother calling him when he was out sailing, but I could get him when he was back and might be ready to talk more."

"I'm sure you feel the same way about this as I do, that we don't want to bother him, just know when the right time might be to connect."

I nodded my head in a yes nod to try to influence Josh's acceptance that he was just helping make a simple connection.

"That's it, that's all I want. It won't be a bother for Mr. Reeves since we're already talking (this lie didn't bother me a bit), so there's nothing for you to feel uncomfortable about," I said, doing my best to influence his mind to do what I wanted.

"So, is that okay with you?" I asked at the same time as now extending the banknote to him.

Again, seeking to answer affirmatively for him, I said, "Here's my number," and handed him the notecard I had already written out.

"Okay?"

"Yeah, sure, okay," he said.

Music to my ears.

"And, the boat is out now, right?"

"Uhh, I don't think so."

I just starting walking toward its berth.

It was there, moored.

I just stared at it. When, how did it get back?

Now Josh was staring at me.

"Oh well, unh, wrong. I guess."

"Thanks, Josh. I'll look for that call."

I gave a little wave and left. How did this happen, I thought to myself. Time to see what cards Mr. Hand was holding.

SIXTEEN

I MADE MY now familiar way back to the Floridan office building. I parked in the lot this time, feeling comfortable and kind of acquainted with the place's routine. I needed to check on the black car to make sure I wasn't waiting in vain. In I went and right to the elevator. Punched the button for the parking garage. I walked rather briskly through the assembled vehicles and spotted the car. Neither the gold nor cream cars were there. I walked back to the elevator and just as I reached it, the bell pinged and the doors opened. A man walked out and we practically walked right into each other. He was as startled as I was, said 'ump, sorry' and made an abbreviated sidestep and continued on his way. Not even a backward glance. I was a little surprised at how the blood was pounding through my chest and head. By the time I got to the first floor it had subsided, but only by about half.

The short walk to my car helped bring me back to mostly normal. I clicked the key over to auxiliary, slid the windows down, turned the key back to neutral, then sat for a minute with the windows down and looked toward the sun, which had already passed its high point for the day. It was getting to be later in the afternoon now, past the customary departure time, and maybe they had all gone somewhere together. How long would I be waiting?

Finally, the black Mercedes pulled out of the parking garage. As I have done before I slid out into the street and began to follow. It started easy this time too, following the main traffic flow. After about twenty minutes he changed lanes to his left. No signal. I kept where I was. In six blocks he pulled into the left turn lane. I had dropped back by several more cars, dragging my feet a little. He turned, and I would not be in his rear view, if he had been looking.

I adjusted, changed lanes, made it to the corner and turned. Ahead of me I saw the black form make a turn to the right. It was the beginning of a residential area. I accelerated but not recklessly. I took the same right turn and was happy to again see the car still ahead. A left turn this time, and he was getting far enough away that it was getting possible that I could lose him. I came around the turn. No car in sight. The houses here were quite nice. Higher end. But not high, high-end, not sprawling mansions. Big yards, nicely separated. This street was only about two blocks long, and as I got closer to the end, I saw taillights stop shining just ahead and to my right in an open garage. I slowed and pulled to the curb. Seemingly unhurried, the open double car garage door slowly descended. I started forward again and drove beyond the house, catching the address out of the corner of my eye. Two more houses on the right, then a street turned again. If there were any markers noting street names, I couldn't spot them. A nice, older, well-established neighborhood, where everyone knew just where they were supposed to be. At the next intersecting street I turned around and went back.

From the first pass I knew where to look for the house address, and with just a glance confirmed I had it, and continued apace back along the path. At the turn that had gotten me to this street, I spotted the stone marker at the intersection giving identification to the street name. Nice, not the usual thin metal placard street sign atop an ugly steel post. And when you did spot the marker, you could find your way. I traced the return path out of the residential area and found a place to stop. Punched up some access on my phone, did an address search, and got a name. John Hand. Okay, Mr. Hand, I've got you.

SEVENTEEN

WITH THIS ONE in hand, I wanted to make the most of it, but it was too sunny and bright out, so I'd have to wait awhile, for my preferred setting, evening. Waiting wouldn't come easy, but it would be the right way to pursue this track. But that didn't mean I had to sit in my car twiddling my thumbs. I made my way back to the main traffic thoroughfare, stopped, and made sure I knew what the intersecting streets looked like, noting the types of buildings and businesses, so I could find my way back, even in the dark. Then I cruised on, looking for something interesting to help pass some time. A likely looking spot caught my eye, reeled me in. A building painted in cool sky blue and bright Caribbean colors, brilliant orange and yellow hues, welcoming me to this place that noted 'Great Cuban Food…and Drink'.

I went in, immediately exchanging the still outdoor warmth for a nicer, moving air warmth native to ocean islands. In fact, the air movement was generated by multiple overhead fans mounted to the ceiling instead of by the windward/

leeward ocean breeze flow, but it was welcome all the same. The interior was welcoming, not plush, just right to recall many beachside relaxations.

"Yes," I would start with a drink, in answer to the question that came with a gentle southern lilt.

"A mojito, please." I'll have to watch myself with things to do later.

I started with camarones. Their preparation made a fantastic flavor sensation, hot peppers, ginger, and just-right thickened coconut milk. This helped with the mojito.

"Yes, yes, thank you, a second mojito."

The ahi tuna and avocado dish that followed almost pushed me over to a change of plans, to decide that I'd rather be just having this food and drink, and this is something I need to watch out for because sometimes the pull of indolence is strong. But, I maintained.

I was taking it slow, and by this time several other folks had arrived and left, but the service seemed to gear itself to the pace of the patrons, and they clearly were comfortable with a patron who enjoyed the slower international style service and meal pace.

I ordered a beer, not the perfect match for what I was eating, but I could draw it out much longer than anything else. I finished. I couldn't see how to drag it out any longer.

Outside the light was fading, but wouldn't depart just yet. I walked up the block. It was good, to help settle my lovely meal, and because I liked to look at things naturally anyway. I looked in the windows of the small shops that had already locked their doors for the night. I like to observe buildings, particularly looking to find nice architectural detailing, and there was a little bit to be found here, around some doorways and over some windows. But nothing remarkable. Sometimes you find a location with buildings that have fantastic detailing, finishes around doors, building corners, cornices, window treatments, that are so finely crafted that these details often seem to impart personality to their host, putting to shame other buildings that do not live up to the imagination and effort displayed by even one such fine doorway. Streetscapes and doorways of Paris and Rome always come to mind, followed by other European cities. Savannah has fine examples. So does New York, a detail here, a doorway there, and they are a delight to find and match against the otherwise overwhelming industriousness of most buildings.

The right level of dusk, heading off into night's darkness, was settling as I reached my car. I am ready.

EIGHTEEN

I PULLED AWAY from the eatery, where the cool blue and bright oranges were now equally enveloped by dusk turning into night. After a few blocks I pulled off into an unobtrusive shadow. I had what I laughingly refer to as my stealth kit. Seldom leave home without my stealth kit. My kit contains dark pants, a dark long sleeve tee shirt, dark athletic shoes, and dark gloves. There's also a dark hat that can be pulled down so far as to cover my face, but I typically only use that when it's cool, or very dangerous. Wearing such a hat when it's warm can be attention getting. The same might be said for a long sleeve t-shirt, when it's warm. This t-shirt can be pulled up to my elbows, a closer to normal appearance. Anyway, I say laughingly because it makes me chuckle to myself because I can't help it—when I think about my stealth kit, I conjure up the image of the Pink Panther's stealth kit with the embroidered glove with the pink 'P' to be left at the scene of the jewel robbery. I wish. The image of a jewel thief remains a thrilling and romantic image. The change into my gear barely took two minutes.

I had no trouble finding my way back. I nodded to the silent stone street marker and went slowly, at a respectable residential street driving pace, past the house. There was light showing inside, but not bright. Past the two houses further down I again turned around the corner and stopped at the point where the house on this corner stopped, and its backyard began. The age of this residential area had permitted the landscaping to mature, so although I wasn't obscure to anyone looking, my stopping spot had some visual limitations. I didn't hesitate. Upon stopping, I got out, closed the door firmly but gently, and started walking. Once I turned the corner I would be just someone out for a walk. I walked at a quick pace. I was already moving gracefully and quietly. I have always been athletic. Might have liked at one point to be a pro tennis player. I like golf too, but the thought of driving off the tee at 111 mph through that narrow corridor of unprotected people never felt comfortable to me. So, I moved well. Also had good reactions to how my feet felt as they touched the ground, instantly sensing whether the ground was soft, or firm, or whether I was starting to step down on an impediment. My step was adept and instinctive. On grass, or dirt, or hard surfaces. Then there were floors. I learned early on, and the hard way, about floors made with wood. Joists and sheathing. About their ability to creak at the wrong time, and place. Most floors in Florida were just concrete on grade, with little likelihood of squeaks. But you must beware giving too little caution. Didn't know if I'd be treading floorboards tonight.

In keeping with the age of the area it had been built without sidewalks adjacent to the roadway, probably intentionally to promote the rural image and the spaciousness of the lot layout. I left the roadway and strode on top of the grass lawn directly to the side yard of the house. There was a four-foot tall wooden fence and a gate. I could easily boost myself over the fence, but why make it hard? I tried the gate latch, grasping as much of the mechanism as possible with both hands to prevent any clanking of the parts. The latch moved easily, I moved the gate enough to slide through, and placed the gate back almost to its closed position, but left it just that little bit backed off and not latched in case it would benefit me later.

There were a couple of windows on the side of the house but they were dark. I crouched lower for each, letting my eyes glide along just above the window sill level trying rapidly to focus and identify anything behind the glass. The first one was draped, so only the back of fabric showed. I coursed along in alert mode, geared toward spotting and identifying any threat. I reached the house corner, crouched low, both making me a smaller target and offering my head and eyes at a different latitude than upright eye level to anyone who might be looking my way.

What I could see around the corner was all inanimate, so I proceeded. From this vantage point it was clear that the rear of the house was basically a big squat U shape, with the far side away from me having the longer leg of the U and extending farther into the back yard than the leg I was on. In between the legs of the U was an enclosed pool, typical for Florida. The enclosures are screened-in areas, structural, attached to and part of the house—screened to try to keep the bugs at bay. The rear wall of the house that I was alongside was the top portion of this leg of the U and had two large windows, and unlike the windows on the side, were not draped, and from the interior afforded expansive views out to the nicely landscaped rear yard. There was only a very soft, low glow of light visible in the first window. I carefully raised my gaze above the sill level, as before, and looked in. This was evidently a master bedroom area, spacious, with nice furnishings. There were a few artworks on the walls that I could see, but they were seemingly just unimaginative reproductions or prints. The light appeared to be filtering through from another part of the house, this room was not itself lit. A room with lights on offers more protection for the would-be spy, it is more difficult to clearly see someone outside when they are trying to be unseen. If someone were gazing out of a dark room, then anything showing up in that view screen is easier to identify. But both lighted and unlighted windows deserve caution. The second window looked into the same room and offered no more insight.

Next came another corner as the exterior wall returned into the center of the U, to the edge of the enclosed pool. The area is lit with very soft, low light, and the pool itself was illuminated. I love water, and pools lit with that underwater light shimmer at night and are very beckoning, but ending up in this pool could only be a problem I knew I didn't want. I assessed the rear wall of the house, recessed inside the bottom of the U. There were windows and sliding doors that looked out onto the pool area. I took more time at this spot, staring hard into the house to the limit allowed by the light and the glass configurations, staring to see if any other eyes might be staring back my way. None were evident, so I took a breath and moved alongside the screened enclosure toward the far side. My goal was to reach a breezeway that was approximately central to the far leg of the U, and that separated a portion of the structure from the final portion of the structure on this far leg of the U, and that might have been an addition that extended this end of the house. The breezeway was roofed, the roof connecting the two portions of this far leg of the structure. I reached the breezeway and ducked into its darkness, which offered some protection from being spotted by the home's occupant. The breezeway had two doors, both about at the center and each going or coming from a different section of the house. The doors were opposite one another and both had an upper window section with a solid bottom section, so I had to look into both to see what might be revealed or be revealing. The door going into the rear extension part was draped. The door going into the more front part was not. The relative darkness of the breezeway made looking into the window easier. The front part was the garage, and the black Mercedes sat in the center of the garage, alone.

Entering the breezeway I had noticed several dark shapes hanging from hooks just beyond the centered doors, toward the other end of the breezeway that opened onto the far side yard. I had assumed these would turn out to be lawn furniture or some such. Instead they were large duffel bag like things, that, when I was close enough, I realized were, in fact, sail bags, for carting, stowing, etc., sails for a sailboat. There were three hanging, all open, as if they were being aired out. They were empty. I went to the far end of the breezeway, which was completely out of the light from the enclosed pool area, to be sure I knew what the full layout of the structure was and was about to start following along the far outside dark wall to circumnavigate the extension when an air conditioner hum that becomes part of your accepted background noise and therefore unnoticed, shut off. Suddenly it was quite quiet. Then I heard a muffled voice.

I backtracked into the breezeway by the door with the draped window and could tell the voice was coming from there. But there wasn't much to try to hear. It wasn't a conversation, just a short sentence, then quiet, then another short group of words. It couldn't be a television or radio, since those mediums couldn't stand this much silence. It seemed someone must be there. I moved closer toward the pool lights to see what might be. Looking carefully around the corner, there was a through-the-wall type air conditioning unit. Apparently, the extension was not connected to the main system of the house. Just then it kicked on again, and made me jump. I shook my head, because it was natural, on for a while, off, but it startled me nonetheless. No more discernable voice sound could be heard. But then a louder sound took over. A door opened, then shut again rapidly. It was a door on the side of the extension. The doorway opened onto a walkway leading back past the breezeway to a doorway into the pool enclosure, just fifteen feet from where I was. I didn't even hear footfalls on the walkway's paving stone sections, but I was already shrinking back along the breezeway's extension wall, but couldn't move quickly enough to the far end and escape.

The driver of the black Mercedes walked past the breezeway opening, in only quarter profile or less. He continued through the door into the pool enclosure, snapped closed a lock with practiced movement once inside. I watched him walk toward the enclosed rear wall of the main structure of the house, slide open a door, enter and slide the door closed without looking back from the way he had come. Another normal movement. I breathed again.

With the Mercedes driver, Mr. Hand, back in the house, the best move was to resume the circumnavigating the extension excursion I had almost begun a few minutes ago. The far outside wall had no windows at all, but did have a second through-the-wall air conditioning unit. Carefully around the farthest corner then along the rear wall of the extension, which had two large windows, both draped. No light appeared to be within. However that was not conclusive, maybe they were just good drapes. Now I returned to the portion of the extension facing into the rear yard, facing into the center of the U and potentially visible from the pool and house. At this distance, although not great, it was just further back enough that seeing the windows of the main part of the house through the pool enclosure was tricky.

I carried a small pair of good binoculars with me, part of my stealth kit, so I looked through them to see. I could see well enough into the house, but did not spot the occupant. There were three large windows on this side of the extension, plus the door, which was like the two other doors I had encountered, a window section on top and solid section below. All these windows and the door's window were draped. The windows and door of the extension appeared to have been meant to provide a visual connection to the rest of the house and pool, and that connection was blocked for some reason at this time. I proceeded cautiously, checking each obscured opening, but with furtive looks up toward the house. The door was not only draped, there was a padlocked hasp attached on the outside. Just as I turned away from looking at this, my eye caught movement inside the house. I dashed for the relative protection of the breezeway, thus completing the circumnavigation of the extension. Protected by the garage corner portion of the breezeway, I watched as another man followed Mr. Hand into the pool enclosure area, where they stopped at an outdoor bar setup, very nice, got drinks, then started to sit down in comfortable looking lounge chairs at the house-side edge of the pool. Before sitting, the second man put his drink down then shrugged off the sports jacket he was wearing. Shoulder holster. Occupied. They were far enough away, the hum of the through-the-wall air conditioners, and the ubiquitous pervasive hum of other, probably central air conditioning units, throughout all of south Florida, conspired to prevent any significant eavesdropping on the conversation, except for the occasional burst of short laughter or expression that characterizes most male to male conversation. I stayed positioned for some time, watched them get refills, settle in again, and considered my options. I wanted to break into this locked room. I think I know what's inside. But these guys are too close.

Wait, for what, one hour, a couple hours, see if they went somewhere and weren't so proximate? I had dealt with the shotgun-toting night guard, but having a shotgun leveled at you is still a little unsettling. These guys wouldn't hesitate if they caught me breaking into the locked room. I didn't have enough for Detective Ramirez to act on. Maybe the time for the break would be when the black Mercedes left for the office. It wasn't going to be comfortable walking away when I thought there was a good chance I had located Mr. Reeves. Then there was the shoulder holster and who knows what else, maybe more shotguns. Knowing that the guys surrounding this deal were willing to shoot first and sort it out later made me think this was the most I was going to be able to do here tonight. As good as I am at night, tomorrow seemed like the right choice. So, after quite a long while of crouching and waiting, in case they drank themselves into a stupor, or they ventured to the extension, or maybe Shamu jumped out of the pool, I went out the far end of the breezeway, turned toward the front of the house along the far outside wall of the garage, along the driveway, and out to the roadway and headed toward my car. I noted the car parked in the drive, Lexus, gold. Mr. Barton, at least, was carrying. As warned, here was notice that they were armed and dangerous.

NINETEEN

I WAS READY to go early. But I had to wait. That didn't make me happy. Black Mercedes man Hand would arrive at his office after ten. That told the time he would leave his house. No point in going to his house until the time I calculated he was gone. I'd find out soon enough when I got there because I was primed for action, one way or another. I didn't like the waiting, but I liked the way I felt. There was purpose to my actions today. I knew what had to be done. The time came. I headed for Mr. Hand's house.

I drove onto his street and made a pass by the house. The garage door was up and the Mercedes was just pulling out. With the quick glance that was all I was afforded I saw that the car had two occupants, two men in the front, driver and passenger. They pulled out of the driveway and onto the street and went the opposite direction from mine. I continued on my direction, turned the next corner as I had done before, watching the receding rear of their car as far as I could until my turning eliminated them from sight. I quickly stopped and turned around to go back, but edged back into the intersection so as to see but not be noticed. Their car was already out of sight. I turned and drove back down the street, noted the now closed garage door, then went almost to the end of the street before easing the car about one more time, then drove back to his house. I stopped before reaching the driveway, kind of straddling the lot line area between his garage side property line and the adjoining property. If someone were looking it might be indefinite which property I was visiting. But this visit needed to be done, so I launched right into it. Maybe he was keeping fresh fruit refrigerated in the extension portion of the house with those air conditioners running. And the padlocked hasp. Probably not.

I walked up the lawn toward the house, toward the garage side. If you duck your head down, you may think that you're in stealth mode, but you really aren't. I didn't bother, just walked right toward my target. I did feel a little better when I reached the garage and continued past the front plane of it, moving toward the breezeway and then the extension. When I got to the breezeway opening on this side I did slow and look around the corner, but I had already convinced myself nobody was left home, and that's what I wanted besides, so it was easier to just act like because it's what felt right and what I wanted, that was how it would be. Nothing was visible in the breezeway. Not even the formerly hanging sail bags were there. I continued on along the outside wall of the extension toward the rear, around that segment of the house exterior, then was at the corner that looked back toward the pool enclosure area and house. I stopped here and focused my attention toward the main part of the structure. Still easier to be seen than for me to see, but I appeared to be alone here. I looked down along the extension wall to where the door was and could see from the corner that the padlock had been removed and the hasp was unlatched.

Time to move, and move to the door I did. I grasped the door handle, turned it, and the door opened. I slipped inside but did not fully close the door. If I was going to be trapped, it would happen. The interior was pretty much what might be anticipated, a guest quarters of sorts, with an open area, a small kitchen and bar area, which would make a nice guest setup. There was a TV. There was an accommodating bathroom. It was a nice suite-like area. There was no one there. Had it been a guest suite, or had it been a containment cell? I was practiced at looking, trying to find something useful. I didn't rush, but I did move quickly. There was water and some milk in the small refrigerator. Also a part loaf of bread and some cheese. There were some dishes in the dishwasher, not full, dishes yet to be cleaned. Not a lot of staples in the small kitchen's cabinets. A coffee maker on the countertop. There were liquor bottles in the bar. But no wine bottles. If this had been a prison for a wine drinker, the conditions were obviously barbaric. There were no clothes in the bedroom closet. There were toiletries in the bathroom. If someone had been kept here, it would have been comfortable enough, if that can ever be true of confinement with freedom denied. I looked through the still draped windows at the meeting of the drapes in the center to see if anything was moving outside. Didn't seem to be. I went out the door, closed it, left it like I had found it.

I turned into the breezeway and looked into the window in the top part of the door, saw that the garage was empty. Just as I left the breezeway on the far side yard side and headed for my car, the phone I had carried with me in my pocket began to vibrate. This was the phone that I had given the number to Josh at the yacht club. He was the only one who had this number. This wasn't my regular phone, but it was one of my tools that I commonly acquired to use in just this way, for contact when I wanted it, from whom I wanted. I was pressing the answer button as I opened my door and got in. Saying 'hello' as I started the car, and 'hi, Josh' as I drove off.

Barton and Cardenas had just arrived at the yacht club, and in mere moments had departed with the sailboat.

"No Mr. Reeves?"

"Nope, just the two of them."

"Okay."

"I know it's not quite what you asked me for, but…"

"No, no, Josh, this is great, you did terrific, great, thanks. This is helpful. Please let me know what else happens, okay?"

"Okay, I will."

"Thanks, thanks very much. Bye."

Something is up.

TWENTY

THE CALL FROM Josh about Mr. gold car and Mr. cream car taking the boat out heightened my already rising sense of urgency. Something is going on. If they've already taken the boat out from the yacht club, my best destination would have to be the boatyard. And now. And quick. And it was already turning into evening, with lots of traffic heading home for the day. My grip on calm slipped a little bit.

The first half mile went pretty well. Everyone was moving along intent on their own satisfactions and the traffic lights cooperated. But it was inevitable to run into heavier traffic, and I did. Slowing, slowing, keep moving, even if it's slow, I was urging. Go, go, go, you've got the light, keep it going. I was contained and working on creating positive energy. We kept moving. No point getting myself worked up. This is city traffic. There are no magic expressways hiding their entryways behind billboards or down low trafficked streets. Wishful thinking. We kept moving. Until we stopped. But the impeding light shortly changed its color and gave us permission to move on despite the final yutzes who had to push their way through the intersection after yellow, holding on to the tail of the car ahead as if their closeness gave them absolution instead of condemnation as tailgaters. But my traffic line was moving once again. A coordinated serpent capable of mostly straight-ahead movement. Then a stretch where traffic thinned and speed increased, increased, this is good, free to run free at last, until the brakes required hard application. Stop. Then slowly into forward momentum again.

This process can be maddening, but we do it daily. Twice daily, for lots and lots of people. I was glad I didn't do it twice a day, but that was fleeting comfort because I was doing it now. Slow, slow, slow, so long as the slow is as steady as possible, slow is better than stop. Another break, another chance to accelerate, another hope for more continuous movement, a flash of hope to break free and run like the wind...then brake. But I was almost to the turning that would allow me to exchange the well-traveled road for the slightly traveled. With an accompanying burst of acceleration I turned into the beginning of the industrial area leading to the boatyard. If there would be traffic flow here, I should be moving counter to it. People should be leaving this part while I'm dashing into the breach. The pace picked up, and I came close to matching the streaks of speed I obtained when following the black and gold the first time, the low rise industrial buildings flicking by. I got within sight of the boatyard, slowing to a merely rapid pace. Nothing was visible in the front, and the gate was shut.

I parked where I had before, and hoped for a safe return as I set out on foot. I circled through the property adjacent to the boatyard, where the last time I had been here I was running, and holding a shotgun. I hastened but didn't run. When I got to the end of the fence at the low wall I tried to assess what was and what might be in front of me. The half-light of dusk had fully engulfed the players and the setting for this drama. As before, I entered onto the boatyard property and dashed to the building wall and edged along it toward the corner that would open to the hidden scene of the rear of the building and the dock area. Had the sailboat arrived already? I was assuming this was its destination. Would the black car be here, and with what as cargo?

I reached the corner. I would be exposed to the rear, visible and vulnerable to anyone coming from the front. That's just the way it was going to be. I crouched low and tipped my head around the corner. The black Mercedes was there, with its trunk standing open. The crew was already working at the conveyance of other sail bags from the dock to the side of the car. I couldn't see, but I wondered if there was a fully stuffed sail bag in the trunk waiting to be exchanged for the bags being offloaded from the sailboat, standing at port at the dock. I wasn't certain in the rapidly darkening twilight, but I thought I could pick out the golden lettering on the stern of the sailboat, of S at the beginning, the round of O, less round letters in the middle, B and R, finishing with the sharp point of A and more rounded letters, D and a concluding O. SOMBREADO. Sure looked like it. I had looked it up after the first time I saw it. I had been close, it did come from sombra, shadow, and it meant shady. Was this just an ironic reference, an inside joke?

The unloading work continued, then two of the crew dropped the loads they carried and turned to the open trunk. My bet was that whatever weight of load they had brought in, the heaviest bag was going to be going for one last sail. The two crew grabbed on to something in the trunk and lifted. It was heavy, but they were obviously strong, and one last sail bag emerged from the trunk. My phone tugged in my pocket. Decide. Answer or ignore. I turned back and ran for separation from the rear boatyard activities. The slowly darkening surroundings didn't contain enough background noise to confidently disguise a phone conversation. There were some low motor noises, a small runabout or perhaps a sailboat under auxiliary power but it wasn't going to be enough to cover me. I had looked at the display before running and knew it was Josh. It was the only one it was supposed to be, and he was calling. Why? I engaged the device and spoke low, 'Yes Josh?'

"Hi, they just came back in."

"What?"

"They've just come back, just now, they're just starting to tie up."

But...but... My mind said, but I didn't.

"The boat is here. Uh, hello?"

"Yeh, yeah. Sorry. They've come back in...and you're looking at them? They're back?'

I had to phrase it out so I didn't say what I wanted to say which would have been 'What? Are you sure, are you sure? How can that be?, I'm looking at the boat right now, maybe it's a different boat, go look, are you sure?'

"Uh, yes, yes, that's what I'm telling you. They've come back in, tied up, and, they look like they're ready to leave already. I thought you wanted to know."

"Okay, yes, yes, thank you."

This phone call was puzzling, but there were more things at hand to deal with. I moved as quickly as I could back to my former cloaked observer viewpoint and took in the scene. The sail bag from the trunk must have been left on the ground for the few moments of the phone call because two of the crew were just hauling it up off the ground, and heading for the dock. And at the dock, the sailboat still sat there. Josh had called me and said the boat had arrived back at the yacht club. But even in the now approaching dark, here it was, practically right in front of me. The name, the look, when I looked it over earlier, even as dusk was turning certain sight into ill-defined shapes and images, I was sure it was the sailboat. They and it were right here in front of me.

But the crew was readying the boat to go out. I had to do something. I stepped back from the corner one more time and took out my phone.

I couldn't overpower them, I couldn't sneak in, even in the darkness, in an attempt to either rescue or decipher whether the sail bag needed rescuing. But if what I thought was going on was going on, leaving on the sailboat would not be best for that sack of cargo. I know I have to do something I repeated to myself. So, I just strolled around the corner and into action. The first guys who noticed me did a kind of double take, obviously not expecting, perhaps not even imagining, that an outsider would just appear and intrude into their midst.

But the looks of surprise barely had time to become thoughts before I walked up behind the Mercedes driver and said, "Hi, Mr. Hand. How's it going?"

He turned, and there was no look of surprise on his face. Just a hard glare that bore right into me. It was obvious this guy wasn't an amateur at this, wasn't caught with his hand in the cookie jar. This was a guy who made his business being hard, doing business in, uh, alternative ways and wasn't the least bit concerned about this unexpected appearance. This guy looked tough. Just then, a face appeared that had a sketchy familiarity to me. A face seen only for a moment, in darkness, a face memorable for the circumstance of the surprise meeting and the rapid parting, a face memorable for a tight, mean smile. My shotgun buddy said to Hand, 'This is the guy that was on the dock'. Now Hand's tougher than rivets look turned into a wry smile, with a hint of relief. Probably I was a loose end that he had wondered about, and now that loose end was going to be tied up, probably figuratively and literally.

"Who are you?" he asked directly to my face. "What are you doing here?"

"Oh, I was looking for something," I answered in a smart-alecky way that I have a tendency to do when I know I need to summon my own toughness and my own strength of resolve. In other words, when I'm in trouble. It might not be the kind of response that lowered the temperature on a potentially explosive situation, in fact, it frequently seems to turn up the heat a bit more, but, it serves as my can of spinach to set me up to muscle my way through.

"Okay, well, you found something."

He didn't seem at all bothered by the Popeye the sailor man music playing somewhere.

He motioned to smiley who grabbed me, and just as I was about to flex my bicep other hands grabbed me from behind. So much for that. The hands and forearms and elbows escorted me to the sailboat and plopped me down in the cockpit. Two others of the crew carried the heavy bag onto the dock, gripping tightly to the fabric at either end and lugging the load, then plopped it too down inside the stern end of the hull.

Hand walked onto the dock and stopped by the side of the boat.

I couldn't help myself.

"We're going for a twilight sail?" I asked merrily.

"Sorry, I'm not going out with you," came the reply, followed by a motion to his men onboard. He turned and walked away.

TWENTY-ONE

AFTER THE TWO GUYS had lugged the sail bag, maybe body bag would be a more appropriate description, into the cockpit, one came over and took up an in-my-face guard position. If I yelled or tried to jump overboard, it seemed certain he could get me faster than I could manage any action of my own. One of the other crew stepped into the cockpit and went to a spot where there were attached seats with seating cushions, lifted one of the seat/cushions and opened a storage bin that was built in below the seat. He pulled a spool of line out and with a flair accompanied by a twisted smile of enjoyment, pulled a five-inch stiletto from his pocket and flicked it open as his eyes settled on mine. He sliced off a length of line, walked over to me with the stiletto held casual-like in his hand, pointed the very pointed and sharp looking blade at me, and made a gesture of a little twirl. "Turn around," he said without saying a word. I half turned, a brave gesture of defiance. The result was the same. My hands got a quick wrap, behind my back. So now if I jumped out, I could only use my legs to tread water or swim. I thought that I wasn't likely to be afforded that much opportunity anyway. The stiletto *spoke* again, 'Sit down' it said, by just the simplest downward movement of its wielder's wrist. With the cargo, such as it was, onboard, the three of the crew were remarkably quick about releasing the tie lines, and off we pushed from the dock. No lifted cocktail or beer to 'let's have a fun sail'. I like water, but it seemed that it wouldn't be long before I was going to be more up close and personal with it than I was going to be happy about. I hadn't even thought yet about whether I would meet the sea with a bump on the back of my head, an extra lead weight in me, or just sliced open like a tuna for chum.

I barely had time to shudder at my own thoughts when the darkness that had now engulfed us blazed into the light of day. Or at least the light of powerful spotlights. From the two large police boats that materialized from the darkness blocking the way and making my pulse surge. With relief. Oh, these guys are good. Their appearance was so sudden and so completely supernatural that two of the crew guys who were sitting didn't even get to their feet. The third guy was standing, and upon the blockade he simply released his hold on the sheet allowing the sail to lose its fill of air, and the sail sagged into uselessness, and so did he. In rapid succession police with guns drawn joined us onboard and with their commands to drop to knees I said, 'My hands are tied', followed by, 'You should look inside that large sail bag'. For my effort, I got a snorted 'Huh', an acknowledgment form of 'Huh', but nothing else.

By now it was getting crowded on the sailboat, but there was room to see one officer crouch down to the zipper on the bag while another stood just behind him with split attention, watching the rest of the activity mixed with downward looks to see what his compatriot might be getting into. Then the crouched officer bent low over the bag, maneuvered something that was out of my sight, then spoke loudly enough to be heard, 'We need some medical help out here, one of the passengers'. The police boats had already formed a floating platform maneuver, with one on either side of the sailboat, tying all three of the craft up as if one. The three crew members were offloaded, all to one of the police boats, perhaps leaving the other free for pursuit if needed. One of the police officers that I assumed had the most medical training joined the two officers standing over the sail bag and began manipulations to the form inside. In only moments he spoke into his communicator, and as I had been left just kneeling, but unattended, the message was clear, we need to get this person ashore. It was only now that any more attention was paid to me.

"Gee, sure nice to see you guys."

"One of those guys has a five-inch stiletto, and I don't know what else."

The cavalry had arrived in time.

"Uh, could I get untied?"

TWENTY-TWO

OVER THE NEXT TWO DAYS I spent a lot of time at the police station. I got to give my thanks in person to Detective Ramirez, and to the commander of the cavalry, the rescue mission. Detective Ramirez had managed the apprehension of the black Mercedes, of Mr. Hand, three other crew members, and, tah dah…four hundred and fifty pounds of cocaine in the trunk of the Mercedes and the bed of one of the pickup trucks. There were also a couple bags of Ecstasy tabs seized, for good measure. A good time was had by all, or for all on the right side of this, of course. Lucky for me Ramirez had gotten my call and set things in motion. It was going to take some time to investigate Floridan Capital Partners, and guess what, the other two I had identified hadn't been located yet. With their names and license plate numbers and addresses, the dragnet was on. The police had visited both condominium addresses but as yet hadn't seen any sign of them. Perhaps there had been an arranged all-clear signal that was to be communicated by Hand, because Detective Ramirez had summoned all the manpower needed to stake out all the residences, but no one had shown. But this was just another part of the job for the detective bureau, to follow up and investigate and eventually to mop it all up. Ramirez winked at me when he said, 'But of course, the fun part was last night'.

Mr. Reeves had been heavily drugged, but not otherwise mistreated despite the clear intent to drop him in the ocean. He had come around early that morning and the police had interviewed him, early and often.

It seems that Hand et al. were playing a little bit of a shell game with the sailboats. They varied the way they used the boats. The general idea was that the sailboat at the yacht club was a decoy, a cover. They sometimes would use the exact same sails, with the same registration numbers. They figured that if they were ever spotted and called on it, they could point to the boat at the yacht club, say, look it's not even out, or they could pinpoint where and when it had been out with confirmation from the kids or other staff at the yacht club, who would say—they only had it out for an hour or two or three or whatever time cover they might want. They figured that with the premise of simple short length pleasure sailing, or with no indication that they had ventured out further than the local waters, the sailboat wouldn't draw the attention that a cigar racer or large motor yacht might. They transferred and carried the drugs in using the large sail bags, stashed in the hold. The runs weren't huge, but they were substantial. The size of the runs fit just right into the large luxury aspect of the sailboat. They felt comfortable about the transfers and their subterfuge with the boats. They could say to whoever might have witnessed something, well, they were just mistaken about the name or numbers. With the boat clearly sitting there at the yacht club, it might not convince someone looking at it hard, but otherwise it offered pretty good obfuscation.

Then, sometimes, they would use different numbers on the sails, made up numbers, just to throw uncertainty on any report. Further, they could take advantage of the decoy bit. Again, they varied it, but one of the maneuvers they had confidence in was to send both boats out when they were going to do a pickup from a supply boat bringing the drugs in from somewhere in the Caribbean to an offshore meeting point. On the run back to shore, if they spotted any surveillance, one or the other of the boats could make for either harbor. The shore locations aren't that far apart, so one could feint coming in to one of the harbors, then dip into the other. They never did bring drugs in to the yacht club, too easy to be seen carting it off, even in those sail bags. But they would have if circumstances forced them to. That's also why Mr. Reeves's habit of keeping up the boat himself was useful, the staff at the yacht club goes on board a lot of the other boats moored there for cleaning, general help. But Mr. Reeves didn't use those services—he just used the staff to help with minimal cartage to and from the boat.

As for Mr. Reeves, there were several factors about how he got involved. It started because he has an investment banking business that the bad guys were trying to explore for money laundering the cash they were hauling in. That's how they first made contact. Then they got invited out for a sail as Mr.

Reeves was trying to reel in some business, and the idea of the twin boats got hatched. A little fanciful thinking perhaps, but Hand envisioned himself as captain of a boutique outfit drug runner, so it fit his vision of himself. Even sitting in lock-up, he doesn't mind telling you how smart he is. Anyway, Mr. Reeves started putting pieces together, and got the notion that the reasons they were talking to him weren't the same as why he thought he was talking to them, and Mr. Reeves was not interested in illegal activities. Well, the bad guys also realized their purposes were coming to the surface, and they realized that Reeves was smart enough to have begun to conclude what their activities were, so they snatched him until they could figure out what to do about him. Killing in the drug world is part of the deal, and there's often some leader's 'strategy' behind it. These guys envisioned themselves a little higher on the chain, which of course is baloney, but that's what they tell themselves. They weren't reluctant to kill him, they just needed the right moment to get it done and to protect themselves from what had been revealed and deduced. Despite their own undeserved grandiose notions of themselves, smaller drug gangs like these importers know that they can be found out and that death brings a higher likelihood of investigation that would perhaps lead to discovery, so it's far better to run as quiet and unattention-getting an operation as possible. But they had misread Mr. Reeves and needed to get him out of sight first then concoct the right way for him to disappear in a permanent state.

As Detective Ramirez concluded explaining how these people had gotten involved with each other, I thought to myself, the gang had decided it was time for Reeves to go, and Mrs. Reeves getting me involved had saved him. And once the process of concluding Mr. Reeves's fate was in motion and I showed up in the middle of it, I was going to be an easy add-on. Glad there was a save on that one too.

TWENTY-THREE

I WAS GETTING READY to leave Miami and head for home. I went over to the yacht club to see Josh and to thank him for his help. Since the police had been all over the sailboat docked at the yacht club, there was no point in withholding, but I didn't add a lot more to what had become common knowledge. I was able to tell Josh that he had helped and what he had done was good. He appeared to appreciate it.

Detective Ramirez had the case well in hand now. The two missing partners were still missing. That wasn't really my part of the action and I had already stopped thinking about it.

Mrs. Reeves was extremely grateful. She had her husband back, not too much the worse for wear, and their lives, while not normal at the moment, had a chance of returning to normal in time.

There was satisfaction for me in completing the task, or adventure, or task. There was always a little bit of a letdown when something like this was concluded. I was happy at the good outcome, Mr. Reeves returned safely, kind of pleased at the positive civil duty of running down some *bad guys*, and I had very much enjoyed the thrill of the chase. But it was done. I could stand back and look at it, savor having lived it. But it was done. It was both similar and dissimilar to how I felt when I finished a painting. I felt much the same at the process of creating a painting, starting with having an idea, although often it was just the slimmest of an idea or a wanting to deal with a color or a shape I saw in my head. Then I progressed through one brushstroke at a time, color on white, then color over color, oftentimes struggling at it, working on it, pushing it to turn something that was only an imagined image and making it exist as an artwork. Sometimes the result was pleasing, colors that soothed. Sometimes the static work jumped with action. Sometimes the result was puzzling and made me wonder whether it worked or was a mess. Sometimes those disquieting works were the ones where I most often saw people stand in front of an artwork and look, turn their heads, rest their chin in their palm, elbow to chest, and I could feel them thinking 'what's going on here?' All of these outcomes were rewarding but were felt in different ways. It was similar with my cases. The ones that turned out all okay, like this one, I preferred, of course. The ones that had harder endings, well, you take something away from those too. Sometimes you take away additional knowledge, sometimes a better way of attacking a problem, sometimes you take away a little pathos that makes you appreciate your life and circumstances a little more. With a painting the frozen image of it would remain, and you could turn to that image, see it and recall it. With cases, mostly, you just had the memory of the involvement.

And sometimes a bruise or two.

TWENTY-FOUR

I GOT BACK to San Isabel. I parked in one of my garage spaces and walked around to the gallery. Cathy greeted me and told me that things had been going well, steady traffic, some sales, very good, very typical summertime. She handed me a note, in her writing, and simply said, "This is for you."

Yes, yes, of course, I stay connected, but those that know me well know I can also take off and be gone for bits and whiles at a time, just like the past few days. So, those in the know leave messages at the regular outposts, the gallery being one, knowing that sooner or later the message will achieve not just delivery but also receipt. Just getting this message made me happy. It was from my great friend Hig. 'Hey, coming to see you.' Another drop-in visit. Great fun.

The day was waning, I was tired, I headed home. After a little more than an hour of puttering around, and not really doing anything, I decided that was it for today. Enough. I'm not a stickler for locking my door. First, I control my complex, have friends around, know the neighbors, and am a bit anonymous in this setting anyway. Sure, when I know I'm going to be gone, I lock up. Mostly, or more often than not, at least. Sometimes I'm too focused on where I'm going. And I just don't. It has never hurt me, well, not deeply at least. So, it was very much in character, expecting Hig, for me to leave the front door to my place unlocked, and then to turn in. A contributing factor is that a long time ago, I had to give up on giving a key to Hig because he loses them immediately. We have been friends since college. Even then I was going my own way, adopting a slightly bohemian front for myself, even if it was something of a masking characterization, and got away with it with the artistic pursuits. But I had already been pursuing investigative work, and the combination made me feel, act, and enjoy an underground, counter-cultural, subversive mantle state of mind. Ah, college, and its delusions.

While I used the artist, going-my-own-way persona when it was convenient, I certainly didn't act the image in all aspects. I have always been good at sports. Not great, but quite good. I throw well, baseball, football, Frisbee. I hit it well, golf, tennis. I can even cradle and fling it a bit, lacrosse. Never did try jai alai. So, when it suited me, I played the introspect, painting and admiring beauty. When it suited me, I skulked around, watching, listening, looking. And when it suited me I joined or started a game, whatever the weather, course or participation opportunity. I also liked riding my bike. Bike riding was freedom as a kid, get on your bike and go places. Later it was both great exercise and an opportunity to think, face in the breeze, mind searching for an answer or for some clarity. Good exercise in both instances.

Bike racing was known, of course, but wasn't an opportunity so close at hand to have even made me think about it. I rode for myself. In my version of evolution then, I didn't associate my bike riding with the revelation that would come only a few years later. No, TV was the connector, just catching it in passing one cool summer afternoon, a day when the weather was okay for summer, which I like to be hot, the other seasons can be cool, that's good too, but summer, I like it hot. So this was a day when there was a bit of the summer desertion permeating the air, in fact, it felt a bit like the latter days of August or the beginning of September when you knew the summer was retreating, and school would begin, or fall was coming. So on this summer day, with declination hanging in the air, I discovered the Tour de France. Guys screaming down a mountain descent, leaning into the corners, coming out faster than they went in, then practically flying through the ensuing straight, like grand prix race cars at full throttle in the straights, until they have to negotiate the next, inevitable corner. Magnificent. It was visual for me, and it drew me in instantly. Colors of the riders, colors of the French countryside, and sometimes colors of the Swiss countryside, and the Italian countryside, and more. Colors of the towns waiting anxiously for their moment of glory, and for the towns on the route, it is just a moment of glory as the tour flashes past, like a charged lightning strike, then is gone, but the memory of that brief blast is deeply implanted. The pageantry, the tactics, the superb athleticism. These appeal to me as an artist, to my less gifted athleticism, to my mind, and to my spirit. I was hooked, and I have been very happy to be hooked ever since.

I have been to France, in the blistering heat of summer, sat by the roadside in a little town, watching and waiting like a kid waiting for presents, until the spectacle arrived. See, I get carried away just thinking about it, recalling how it started, and how it inhabits me yet. Vive le Tour.

My mind does this sometimes, just leaps off to somewhere else. I enjoy the reveries, so I am not anxious to draw myself back to where I had been, but, sometimes more directly than other times, I do get back to where I left from. Bicycle.

It is and it isn't a direct connection. One sunny spring afternoon I was throwing the baseball around with some guys. Just enjoying spring. A straight toss here, a pop-up emulating toss there. Just easy, just enjoying the sunshine, being outside, and being young, owning the world. College delusions. A guy was walking a bike on the sidewalk at the edge of the grass lawn where we were throwing the ball. It wasn't my throw or catch, but one of the others overthrew, and the ball bounced right up to the front wheel of this guy's bike. "Little help" came the familiar call. The guy with the bike looked at the ball, took two more steps. Since "little help" is a friendly appeal we all felt universally recognized, and we were all waiting for it, when nothing happens, it is kind of confusing. "Uh, please', rang out a second verse that we aren't really prepared to put forth because one call is all we expect it to take. Now, we've all seen people pick up a ball and launch into an ungainly throwing motion, or awkwardly stride into a ball for an ungraceful kick that can go awry and leads to chuckles, or we've all picked up an errant tennis ball to swat it back to its rightful court and hit the top of the fence with it instead, and with chagrin go, gee sorry, try again. But the universal theme is that everyone responds, and the particularly sports object is put back into play, and mostly it is very forgettable. This wasn't. The guy walking his bike looked again at the ball, now at his feet. He looked out at the beseecher, and just stood there. The beseecher began the slow walk of someone who wasn't receiving expected assistance, the hesitating walk consisting of a step, stop, step, because, again, you expect that 'little help'. You recognize that someone who isn't good at doing what you're doing might make an errant return, so you don't mind having to move, you just expect some kind of return to initiate where you need to move to.

We are now all watching, anticipating the actions we expect. Pick up the ball, throw it back, at least somewhat toward the obvious participants. Yeah maybe it won't be a great throw that's okay, even if it takes ten feet off the retrieval, it's all accepted as part of the ritual. The guy with the bike looks at the ball. It appeared that would be all he would do. But then he bent down and, holding his bike upright with his right hand, he reached down with his left hand to pick up the ball. He got it, stood upright, then held the ball about head high, palm facing forward with the ball in it, and seemed to not know what to do next. He raised the ball in his hand even higher above his head, looked like he was trying to hand it over a high fence to someone on the other side. He apparently realized this wasn't going to work, so he began to transfer the ball to his right hand. His bike crashed over to the ground. Now he had the ball in his right hand, but he was turned away from us, looking at his bike on the ground.

Then he turned back and with a motion like swatting at a fly an arm's distance away, flung the ball.

The guy who had originally been overthrown wasn't that far away now, having continued his stagger step toward the bike guy, in a, well, is something going to happen, step, maybe not, step, maybe, step, slow pace toward retrieval on his own. The flung ball was not closer to him, but the effort had been made. He changed direction and picked the ball up, looked at the bike guy, and I hear him say, 'Uh, bike okay?', to which the bike guy just picked it up and walked it and himself away. The ball retriever turned back to our waiting group of sporting enthusiasts, held his hands out to the side, finished the shrug, then sent a pop-up throw my way. I caught it without drama or hesitation, turned and threw one of my own, and the game of toss was back underway, the experience with the bike-guy a nonissue.

TWENTY-FIVE

, I was walking along a pathway through campus. This was a pretty place. There were plantings of flowers encircling the drip line of trees, bushes, and shrubbery, and occasionally a meandering small stream with a rock bed made its appearance. There were numerous small fountain areas and scattered seating retreats. It made for a nice walk.

Ahead, seated on the low containing wall of one of the fountain bases was the bike guy. He was about the same height as I was, slighter in build. Dark, short, slightly wavy hair. A thin face. He was staring at the ground with his bike alongside him propped against the same wall he was sitting on. With my approaching footsteps, he half looked up. From an almost completely blank look on his face, his expression changed to a kind of sneer, but it was the sneer of a snot-nosed eleven year old who hasn't perfected a really convincing, wall streeter, look down your nose, arrogant facial set. He looked like somebody's little brother who was trying to put up a front when you bossed him around, not that it was right to boss around someone's little brother, but it happens. I'm not put off by such jackasses who have come closer to perfecting that *I'm tough*, or special, or gifted, or whatever mistaken notion they have that causes them to offer such nonsense in the eye contact sizing-up exchange. I'm better than most at presenting a cold stare, in fact, although I just use it to create an effect. So, despite the attempted tough face, whether it was intended for me or was just his mask, I smiled and said, "Hope your bike is okay." I didn't say 'your arm needs some work'. I didn't say 'you know, bikes are for riding, not walking'. His sneer attempt melted instantly, but I was surprised that it was replaced by a decided look of uncertainty, maybe even a touch of sadness. He didn't respond verbally, but his posture took a half-degree turn to slump. I tried again.

"Do you need some help," letting the words drift off and giving only a very slight gesture toward the bike.

Despite the withdrawn appearance he was presenting, he didn't mumble a 'no' and keep looking down. He made a counter move, something not in keeping with the down-trodden demeanor.

He looked up, directly at my face, and said, "No, thanks," with an air of genuineness.

That could have been the end of it. Could have just stated, matter-of-factly, 'okay', and walked on.

Instead, I parried with, "Do you ride a lot?"

His response was resigned but was spoken in the comfort-able way that you use when you talk to friends when you're just sitting around, not an important discussion, just casually commenting on all the world's problems.

"I'm not very athletic. Sorry that I didn't do a good job of getting the ball back to you guys."

Ah, recognition. I had no way of knowing for sure if he had made the association, it had happened in a distant way.

"Oh, don't worry." The response was meant to be neutral, but when I said it, it didn't feel like it was encouraging enough or wasn't thanks enough for someone who, it seems, had had to do something they were almost completely unequipped to do.

I decided to take one more shot at it.

"So, did your bike break down?"

"Oh, no," he launched, without hesitation, "the stay holding the seat at the right height in the seat tube broke, making it impossible to pedal."

Economical description of the problem, delivered with engineering precision.

I had been recounting this meeting to myself, and this is the last I remember of where I was in the telling of the story when sleep enveloped me.

TWENTY-SIX

I WOKE UP. It was dark. Just minutes after two a.m. Heard some very slight rustling. Ah, Hig must have arrived, must be doing his best to settle into the guest suite quietly. Might as well go and welcome him.

I stepped out into the hallway and headed for the guest suite at the other end of my floor layout. The door to the guest suite was open, with no light. I stopped at the doorway and began to reach for the light switch just inside. I was slightly amused, here was Hig being as quiet as possible and I was going to surprise him by throwing on the light, and it would shock him, but, he did wake me up, after all. Before I touched the light switch, a dark figure apparated in front of me and instantly I took a hit right to my chin. It rocked me back into the hallway and into the wall. The figure in black dashed past and headed for the front door. I wasn't hurt but certainly stunned. It took a couple beats to center myself and then pursue the figure. He, it, was already out. I reached the front door in time to see the figure hit the bottom of my wide stairway and fade into the darkness. I almost launched down the stairs like a ski jumper popping onto the track, but a modicum of sense took over. The figure had a good head start, I had no shoes on, and, last, what if the figure hadn't been alone. I wheeled around inside the front door frame and hit the 'all lights on' tab on my control panel. I had overseen all the rehab and remodel on this old building that now housed my gallery and my home, and it was equipped with modern wiring and technology features. Lot of good if you leave the door unlocked. Might as well had just left the door wide open. Well so much for surprising a late-arriving Hig. It was me that got the surprise.

Now started the, well then, what was this about? Random b & e attempt? Something else? I didn't feel the need to draw out a gun. I walked back through the large open space that is entry and living room/great room/dining room. The kitchen is also mostly open to this area so it was easy to see that no one else was in these parts. I crossed first to the guest suite area, opposite from where my study was. To search, I would have to go in, losing sight of anything behind me. The guest suite is that, with its own bathroom within. I entered, swept my eyes around the portion I could see, then quickly turned back to look back to the main area to see if anything emerged from hiding and made a dash for the front door. No movement. I crossed the bedroom portion of the guest suite and went into the bathroom. Nothing. I opened the walk-in closet doors. Abruptly. Nothing. I went out and crossed again the main portion of my place, ducked my head into my study, saw nothing. Two more places to look, the master bedroom and then the laundry room. As I was searching the rooms I was also noting the things, computers, TVs, art still in its places on the walls, those kinds of things. The master was as I had left it, except without the amused anticipation of seeing a friend. Next into the master bath and even with the obscure glass in the shower area I could see nothing was there. Same for the closets. When you come to that last place to look, you are telling yourself it's okay, nothing here. But your heart is going pound, pound, pound of its own accord. The door to the laundry room was closed. It opens inward, so, away from me. I pushed it open. No monster.

Yikes. I felt the adrenaline. Whew. Now the 'what the hell?' started rising higher in me. 'Who the …?'. 'Why the …?'. As almost an afterthought, I crossed to one of the big outside doors and looked out on the deck. The expected and familiar shapes of chairs and loungers greeted me. Nothing out of place. I sat down to think. No solid answer was forthcoming. I did not sleep very well for the rest of the night. I did lock the front door.

TWENTY-SEVEN

AFTER THIS VERY RESTLESS NIGHT, I woke up early. Odd how sometimes it can be hard to sleep when you need to sleep. It was earlier than normal for me, so it was earlier than the automatic start had been set for, so I punched the start button on the coffee maker. I quietly slid open one of the doors to my deck. There is a garage space below me, but from previous years of many different habitations it was clear to me how many inconsiderate morons there are who slam their doors, play 'their' music much too loud, never learned a few basic animal training skills, therefore never imparted to their dogs that all it takes is a few barks to alert anyone who isn't brain dead, and, that really, nobody else wants to know that 'you are here' and that your making noise to assure yourself that you are still alive and ought to be cared about is only in your own head. I slid the door open quietly, respectful of my neighbors and of the greater glory of the quietly unfolding early morning on the far horizon. At peace with the universe.

My deck looks to the ocean. Yes, it is a pretty special way to greet the day. I worked for it. I'm continuing to work for it. It is a wonderful peace, to look out to the calm water, with just little greeting laps at the shoreline, the water and sky both rolling on to infinity. In peaceful moments it can make you feel infused with superpowers. In less peaceful moments, it can influence your thoughts to show you that you have a long way to go to be anything consequential. This morning was at peace, but then last night started to exert a pressure. I turned back inside, got coffee.

With the second cup in hand, I went down my stairs to look around, to see if anything not easily noticed in the night darkness would be apparent with dawning light. Nothing was learned.

I got ready for the day. Shaved, showered, clean and ready to face what might be in store. How else to start the day?

I walked to the street, since it was still early, to enjoy how quiet it could be before most were moving. At the street entrance to my gallery I saw that Cathy was already inside. My hand on the door informed me that it was locked. It was a firm lock, so no jiggle alerted her, but an easy tap on the glass did. Yes, putting my key in might have accomplished the same but a light tap on the window had a more bon vivant, hello to the day and all its habitants feel to it. I was enjoying the light feeling I had. She came to the door directly and blurted, "Are you okay?" My light, happy to greet the day feeling dissipated like morning mist upon the full on emergence of the morning sun.

"Yes, thank you, I'm fine." I held on ever so tenuously to my light feelings.

"Why? Are you alright?" Thud, they left me.

"Well, I'm not sure. Yesterday, after you were here, just before closing, well, not like two minutes before, which would have seemed really odd, but, like twenty or fifteen minutes before two guys came in and looked around, but I just knew they weren't buyers, but of course I thought maybe they were just checking it out like maybe before somebody famous or rich and pretentious might come in like they were the advance team."

I was almost exhausted from listening to just this part. A slight intake of breath and the ride dropped over the next drop. Hang on.

"But then I knew they couldn't be checking it out for any buyer that seemed likely because really they, now not from their dress, they weren't slovenly, but they just looked like, like…"

If you don't have something nice to say… the thought began in my head…

"…like, well, like…thugs."

Ah, thugs.

"Well?" she said, looking concernedly at me.

"Ah, well, you are telling the story," I said. "I don't yet know what to make of it."

"Oh, sure, well then, one of them and I'm surprised to say it, but they both looked kind of the same, but not like twins, just similar looking."

I nodded but the coaster pushed on.

"Then one of them said, 'Buenos dias señorita', very softly, very smoothly, but it felt like there was some menace it, 'is Mr., you,' she half gestured at me, 'here?' Well, you know that even with clients I know, with clients who are purchasers, I'm always a bit protective in saying where you might be."

"I like that about you," I replied, although I only got out the 'I' and she talked over the rest.

"So I don't know why that startled me a bit, but I wasn't as quick to mount my 'I'm in charge' posture, and so I stammered once or twice before I became completely inane you know and I, um, well, just stood there while trying to yell at the inside of my head to get it together."

She stopped. The silence was total. She was looking right at me.

I looked back, and I know I was feeling slightly bemused by her telling of the tale, but I was also appreciative of her completely open demeanor, and of her concern.

"They were polite enough. They looked at me kind of like you are now when I just stood there with my mouth open, I guess it was open, I don't know for sure. Then the one just shrugged ever so slightly, he turned, and they just went back out. They got into a black, expensive-looking car, sorry, you know I don't know cars, or care. All the windows were dark. Oh, well, someone else was obviously with them, because someone was driving. One of them got into the front, the other got in back. So I woke up in the middle of the night thinking about it. Then when I woke up early, it was still on my mind, so I thought I needed to check on things here."

Touching my chin, I wished my alert system was more like hers.

Everything was fine at the gallery. There had been no intruders. Cathy felt better. It seemed right not to increase her level of tension so I just held on to my own tale of last night.

As I walked around the gallery checking that things were okay, occasionally nodding or smiling in concert with Cathy's nod or smile as she moved around the gallery checking things for probably the third or fourth time, I stopped in front of a painting that wasn't mine, a pastoral scene, landscape realism. It was one of Cathy's. Taking in the image, I cast my glance at her across the room. She was tanned and slender athletic. Her blond hair was almost always pulled back in a ponytail, oftentimes sticking out of the back of a ball cap. She painted too and also worked in ceramics. Her painting style was representational and she generally worked on canvases smaller than 2'x2'. Her works in the gallery were a marked contrast to mine, which made for a little variety in our space. She would occasionally discover a young artist that she wanted to give a helping hand to and would hang a few pieces of their work to see what response it got. It helped keep the gallery fresh and inviting. I'm happy that she does this.

She grew up between two brothers. Having been around the three of them, I was never sure who had more influence on whom...or who could be tougher, more dominant. It turned out that she was a little harder edged than suited me. But we had fun for awhile, now we're friends, and she does a good job of looking after me and my interests.

I went outside and all around the building, looking for signs of vandalism or breakage or just something out of place and saw none. I stopped in at the police station and asked if there had been any activity reports or break-ins or any excitement whatsoever. No. Our town is small, and so is the police force. It's an okay situation normally.

I had one more stop to make, Crazy Karl's. That wasn't the shop's real name. The real name is The Beach Shop, but everybody calls it Crazy Karl's. I've found the owner to be reliable, and, the eyes and ears of the town. His shop is an interesting place. He has an ice cream setup on one side and a t-shirt/ beach stuff shop adjacent and connected. You can get some ice cream and wander into the clothes and stuff part to buy a t-shirt. The shop doesn't have any signs saying 'No Food or Drink'. There's also no 'No Shirt No Shoes No Service' signs. The shop, like the owner, projects a laid back attitude in keeping with the location. That's also the first impression you get of the owner, with his long hair and beard and true-to-his-shop t-shirts and shorts beach attire, but when you step up to speak to him, you'll see the intensity in his eyes.

When he introduces himself to someone he says 'I'm Karl'. I know him to be Grigore Karl. To most people in town he is either Greg, or more usually Karl. Tourist shoppers have no need to go beyond this self-identity. Most in town who call him Greg do so because they aren't quite comfortable with how Grigore is really pronounced. He usually responded, pretty much nonchalantly, non-judgmentally, but unenthusiastically, to Greg. On some buoyant occasions when I am efficacious, I'll see him and say "Good morning Grigore" the i a long e sound. I almost always see a brief, very brief, smile crinkle at the side of his mouth. And to a standard, "Grigore, how's it going today?" I think he takes some perverse pleasure in out of the ordinary responses:

How's it going Grigore?

"I'm riding a lightly cresting wave."

How's it going Grigore?

"Crashing to the bottom and sand in my trunks."

How's it going Grigore?

"Dragged out to sea in the undertow."

Some of his replies, with a slight Russian-Ukrainian-Slovakian lilt, hint at what I've found to be a bit of a fatalistic demeanor to his worldly outlook. I do enjoy seeing the outward presentation soften a bit when I see that brief touch of smile. Another greeting I sometimes use is to say Monsieur Gris. His lip curls up just a little when he hears that greeting too.

He is a bit of a local legend, a bit of gruff old don't mess with me guy, the guy who would start telling what was wrong with local, national and world politics at the spark of an invite as simple as 'what's going on?' Despite the bombast, he was a straight shooter. Never has a problem with the health inspector, keeps the shop very clean, pays his taxes—'Oh you don't want those bureaus messing with you, you better believe it'. He always refers to 'those bureaus'. He doesn't say government, big brother or any of the common euphemisms, just 'those bureaus'. I haven't figured that one out, yet. This also adds to my thinking that at some point he was some kind of foreign government agent.

I know him to be a bright guy. We have an easy camaraderie whenever we get together. Running his shop seems inconsistent with other aspects of his persona. He is typically reading several books at a time on foreign policy subjects. Those who do get the chance to know him are accepting of the fact that when you greet him with a simple 'hi' you will just have to see where his reply would go. There was also an unseen side. The hard-luck kid, after being harangued by Karl for a few minutes, usually about larger issues than the kid could see how they might relate to him, despite Karl's insistence that 'you'd better face up to this now', would get five dollars or ten dollars and a little pat on the shoulder, with the soft spoken closer 'you'll make it'.

I get a kick out of The Beach Shop's t-shirt selections, several of which greet passersby in the outside display windows. Karl changes them frequently, and they reflect his take on the world. Today the t-shirt/slogans on prominent display had these messages: 'Laziness kills' in the top line, 'Just more slowly' to finish the wording; 'Error 404, Joke not found'; and, in large letters 'Free Tibet' followed by smaller lettering 'With purchase of another Tibet of equal or greater value'. Karl tells me he makes them up himself.

Just as interesting locally, the t-shirt shop portion of his enterprise sold swimwear among the other goods. The dressing room stalls aren't large, and the draw curtains for changing privacy are as skimpy as some of the current swimwear offerings. All the local girls know it, and perhaps as a result of cable TV, modern communications, youth and easing social values, nobody seems to mind. I've seen this for a long time in

Europe, where girls mostly, would change into swimwear in full view on the beach, and nothing was thought of it. Maybe it was a local rite of passage, but I have overheard many a conversation from groups of the young coming-of-agers that went—'I tried on a hot suit today, and I flashed crazy Karl', which statement would be met with just giggles not shock. Such it was with Crazy Karl.

I found Karl behind the checkout counter of the t-shirt area, it was too early in the day for ice cream customers. I told him right off what had happened. I didn't need to hedge with him. He gave me his full attention, eyes narrowed as he absorbed the tale. At the end, I asked if he had seen or heard anything that might help make sense of this.

"I saw the car, couldn't see who was inside, I watched it drive off."

I don't know how he does it but he doesn't miss much.

"Do you want some help, I'll keep watch if you like?"

Two years ago, in the height of the summer season, Karl had to go away for about two weeks. He told me he needed to go. He said he would need to close the shop. I offered to keep his shop open for him. Cathy helped me, we took turns looking after our various enterprises and kept the summer cash flow going for all. Karl was more than willing to assist both of us. He had our backs.

"Thanks, I don't think there's anything to be done right now."

Karl pushed some stray long hair back over his ear. His longish hair and beard were the same dark brown color, with slight touches of grey insinuating their way in. His beard wasn't long, just full enough that you could lose sight of this fingertips when he scratched it.

"If I see anything, I'll let you know, and when you want help I'll be there."

"Thanks." I gave an upturned palm as a 'see ya' departing gesture and left.

I had a really good time for those two weeks, particularly knowing that it was just for two weeks. I couldn't, wouldn't, do it full time, but it had been fun. I kinda enjoyed the occasional by-chance glimpse into the dressing stalls too.

TWENTY-EIGHT

I WANDERED my way back home. When I got there, the front door was open. It wasn't a surprise because parked in front, looking resplendent and quite at home, was a beautiful, shiny, red Ferrari F430. Hector George Goldman, nee Hig, has arrived. One of the interests we share in our friendship is a love of fast, beautiful cars. Here was an outstanding example. I had a small pang of jealousy, the car was so alluring, so gripping, but it passed quickly. I could have a Ferrari, I can't say 'if I wanted', because I do want one. But it would be very impractical for me. The car would be too easily noticed, and there were stretches of time when I was away, pursuing some case or working on an art project, or just traveling, which I very much like to do. I love going to Europe, the Far East, and many, many places that I have already visited and want to go back to, or that I haven't quite gotten to yet but will. And, I particularly like Mexico—I love warm water. There are just so many places to visit, to learn about, and to use to expand my existence and by extension, my art. It would be a bit of a stretch for me to easily afford a brand new Ferrari, but it certainly was obtainable. Better to travel to Modena and Maranello.

Hig's circumstances were different. I was just thinking about how we first met last night, wasn't I. After I had the hint that he had a technical or engineering bearing, we spent a couple minutes with normal college banter, what classes, food, beer, so on. We did not compare zodiac signs. With each give-and-take, he became a little less guarded and a little more engaging. My initial assessment turned out to be accurate. He was a technology/science/geek crowd member. I didn't mind. I was a sports/outgoing, artist underground subversive pretender dichotomy. He didn't mind. We found we got along. This became beers, burgers, full five-minute in-depth discussions of world situations that needed remedying and that we could supply the answers to that were interrupted and terminated by pretty girls passing within any distance.

New technologies were emerging and Hig had the idea for a better mousetrap. He invented both the medium and the device for a different CD. His version, explaining this only in very simple terms, was a CD that was about the size of a quarter and could be packaged like a roll of quarters. Actually, his first simple explanation to me used comparisons to Necco wafers, but quarters, it's like the same thing. Never heard of it? Yeah, that's because he was already in the sphere of a consortium of electronic producers through his schoolwork, seminars, workshops and so on. They could see what he might be capable of, and they were supportive in looking at new ideas. But his idea came along before the explosion of new introductions of new technology devices and before the manufacturers and marketers learned that the public was dying to try and therefore would buy, anything new and or different. He was part of their community. They knew much of what was being developed and were encouraging about such developments. Yeah, the environment he was in was a little bit like Real Genius. When he was able to demonstrate his product, the manufacturers concluded that it would have meant major manufacturing changes for them, costly, and a different mode than the one they had committed millions upon millions to. They didn't see that the newest tweak to any consumer product would be gobbled up by a public willing to try anything new. They went with safety. They bought all the rights to Hig's product, then put it far back in a storage room somewhere. That's okay, it worked out for him. He got millions. New Ferraris are absolutely no problem for him.

So, we did and still do share an affinity for fast cars. For great looking cars. For exotic looking versions. Actually, we feel the same about supermodels too, but they're way harder to deal with. We read about sports cars, collected sports car magazines, watched races whenever we could, and dreamed about them. We weren't quite there yet, to a place where it would be easy for us to sample the exotic wares of speed and noise and performance, but we started angling toward it. So before Hig became superrich, and before I became less rich but doing really, really well, we, like any sensible persons, took the path of having the experience at car racing camp. There are many locations throughout the country, and we have tried several, that is, the weekend car racing sessions put on by Skip Barber, and others. For a few thousands of dollars you get to man a race-worthy machine and feel the power, the drift, the acceleration, and speed. You also learn about control of the vehicle, in traffic, through the turns, cornering, maneuvering. These skills turned out to be useful to me many times in many situations off the controlled atmosphere of the track. So, attending these race sessions, you get some classwork in, learn what's expected of you and how the course works and the rules to follow, then you get to experience it. From the moment you settle into the cockpit, before, actually, because of the anticipation as well as more than a little bit of anxiety, the thrill is in the doing. You settle into the cockpit, which envelopes you. There isn't a lot of extra space, just room enough to wrap your hands around the steering wheel, to maneuver the gears, and to feel your foot on the accelerator pedal. Yes the brake is there too, and you will need it, and you will use it, but, the first time you are allowed to depress the pedal, to hear the rising volume of sound from the engine and feel the vibration increase, you can't wait for the feeling of being pushed back in the harness against the padded seat and to hurtle into the chase for speed.

Hig is from the north-central East Coast. He is comfortable with the variables of that region's weather. While I love the heat, he will tolerate it for awhile but then needs to retreat for awhile. In looking for a place to settle, although he could have adopted an always on the move jet-set style, his upbringing made him more comfortable to be rooted somewhere. He found a place in the Pennsylvania countryside. You can't call it remote—it's the east coast. It's not like being in Montana.

But it is a little bit out of the bustle. He bought a four hundred acre farm because he liked the space. Over time he had the opportunity to get to know neighbors who were, for the most part, aging farmers, which is also a great problem for our future, for food production and way of life. When these aging, often long-time farm families, reached the end of their ability to manage all of the hard and sometimes harsh aspects of their rugged productive lives, they have few places to turn. Often the younger generation has left behind the hard farm work and headed for city life but they have also left behind the freedom of their ancestors and traded it in for the I want it now world of urban life, often with an unanticipated and self-inflicted loss of individualism. The options for aging farming families frequently comes down to developers, of which there are many, or to the dwindling individuals and families hardy enough to continue the agricultural productivity that feeds us and the world. Don't get this all wrong. Developers provide places to live that we need. This is good and valued. But the change of this basic piece of the backbone of this country, farm production, bringing a loss of those hardened individuals who compete against mother nature at her least tolerable to bring us the things that grow from mother nature at her best and allows the bulk of us to consume, is a loss that makes us lesser in individualism and strength.

Hig was an extraordinary alternative. He acquired the properties of his neighbors when they wanted to sell, at prices that didn't diminish the effort and commitment that they had provided to their landed legacy. He cared for the acquisitions, for the land and what it meant. For the most part, he leased out the right to continue the farming practices inherited with the land to those who still had the drive to undertake this hard and uncertain work but who hadn't been in the right circumstances to have it for their own. This provided a continuity of the farm production and was appreciated within the local community who understood the change and appreciated the continuance of the heritage, even if, perhaps, for just a while.

Hig did make a change or two. I had the distinct honor of consulting, assisting, even at times being up close and personal with the process with lumber and nails in hand, and at times supportive from a distance, with the renovation of an old farmhouse into a modern and contemporary residence, lacking in no comfort, yet having a peaceful coexistence with the land. It retained much of the comfortable, rural ambiance of an old farmhouse, but a farmhouse that was brought into the now with soaring ceilings, large glass expanses bringing the beauty of the farm indoors, skylights bringing in light, a gourmet kitchen, and luxurious bedroom suites. I also helped him with artwork selections for the walls and sculptures, Hig particularly liked sculptures. It was nice that there were several of my paintings throughout the house, and when I visited, it was like seeing a bunch of old friends, a very warm feeling. Both of us were particularly fond of some pieces we found, Native American evocative southwest spirit masks, exquisite, painstaking handcrafted works by an artist out of Moab, Utah. The creation is these life masks where the mask face is covered with small colored feathers hand applied, and then there is the halo of headdress features spiking out to the heavens. Great artworks. Oftentimes when I pass by any one of them, they feel so full of intrigue, so imbued with spirit, that I'm certain the eyes are assessing me. Hig has two, and I have two in my home as well.

Oh, that other change that he made. It doesn't take up a whole lot of space. No, in fact, it is a relatively narrow addition, more than a path, but less than a superhighway, through the cornfields that remain very well nurtured alongside. This change is a twenty-five-foot wide ribbon of asphalt, incongruous in this setting admittedly, but it only minimally interferes with the overall expanse of the property. Yes, you can see it coming. This ribbon allows one of the thrills of Hig's, and my, existence, to pulse through those fields, upon this ribbon that he laid out and surfaced to create his very own two and a half-mile road course. It's not as wide as a grand prix course, but it is a road course, and it is his.

With the racing camp session experiences owned by us, when the opportunity came and his destiny had been manifested, Hig set out to acquire something similar to the scaled-down open-wheel race cars that they use at these tracks for himself. He did. His choice was the Formula 2 style of the 1960's open-wheel Brabham and Lotus Formula 1 and 2 cars. Absolutely gorgeous. These style racing machines were driven in their time by racing greats such as Dan Gurney, Jackie Stewart, Jim Clark, and Graham Hill. Fully race prepared and race worthy, these small missiles can hit triple-digit speeds on the straights and can corner like they are on rails, if you know what you're doing. If you don't, maybe you'll end up out in the corn, ala *Field of Dreams*. He brought it home and starting racing. Then he knew he needed something more, and so, for his ribbon of asphalt through the Pennsylvania corn, he got a red racer, a green racer, and a yellow racer. The better to race with.

We get together every couple of months when it's warm and run 'em. It's great fun. When I arrive at the farm, I have to catch up, to get the feel back a little, for the speed and the performance. Hig has the advantage since he can stay tuned up and does. But after a few laps, we're usually back to even-matched, and we make the most of the races. Admittedly it is a lot of fun to just take a car out solo, to power down the stretches and wind through the turns of the road course. Very grown-up go-kart racing. Or, maybe we aren't so grown up at all. That's okay.

Hig continues this pursuit and has quite a stable now. Along with the three matched open-wheel racers, which make racing fun because if the car performance is the same, it can't be the cars, since their performance and upkeep are all equal, it has to be the driver, there are some other racing options. Hig went out and acquired a dream car, a Shelby Cobra. We both had envied the tales of this car in our respective youths- the name, the performance, the look, the power, the growing legend, the car—Cobra. In the youth time frame, I had found a t-shirt proclaiming Shelby Cobra. My friends didn't know of it, then, or get it, but I did. I loved putting on that t-shirt.

Hig found the car, for sale, a difficult search, to find a true Shelby Cobra, and to reach a selling price. But he had done it. The throaty roar of that vaunted engine rattled through to our cores.

Then, well, it's hard to say he went one better since the car is so unique. Having an authentic Cobra is something. They have been raced on the most famous racing circuits of the world in their prime. Now you might see one in a vintage auto race, and I get why an owner would take the chances with the car in order to have the chance to feel its pedigree and recreate the superiority of the car on the track. But at often more than one million, two million, even three million dollars per change of ownership, it's a lot to chance. So, what may be the next best thing, Hig had constructed three replica Cobras to use on his track. It remains awesome to see that oval open mouth on the front end followed by the wide tracking rear come screaming down the straightaway. I'm one of the few people that Hig lets drive the original, and we have the same fun when we race the replicas.

I bounded up the stairs and found Hig sitting on the deck, with a beer glass at his elbow. It is always fun to see each other again. It is really nice to have a good friend.

A couple of days passed pretty quickly. We hit the local spots, for everything from burgers and beers to fresh seafood and good wine. We drove the Ferrari (before the beers and wine) on some of the less frequented roads around. We exchanged philosophical viewpoints. I told him about my latest adventure and about the surprise of the other night, and that I still didn't know what that was about. He filled me in on some new ideas he was working on developing, and some investments ideas that people were pitching to him. People pitching ideas for him to put his money into happened a lot.

When we get together, we always laugh about some of our old recollections and enjoy planning new ones. Another thing about Hig is that he was a bit of a schlub dresser in college. His style has evolved somewhat, with some good classic elements like designer jeans and expensive polo shirts. At the bottom of this presentation, where in the past there were always dowdy black shoes or garden variety tennis shoes, he has become a Vans aficionado. Yes, among many others, he has a pair of black and white checkerboards.

As all good times must, it was time to go back to our separate pursuits, and so the visit ended. I gave a wave as the taillights headed off, thinking it was fun to visit, and that I was already missing the car.

TWENTY-NINE

WITH HIG GONE, I wanted to, needed to, get down to some business, of one kind or another. There was painting to be done. I wanted to get back to composing, to stroking paint onto canvas, to be completely and utterly absorbed in the creation. It was a powerful, emotional state to be in. It could arise from sheer happiness, joy at making my version of communication. It could emerge out of anger, where I might be practically desperate to secure my view, present it, and anticipate the response. It could come of frustration, or of a state of harmonic complicity with universal powers. It always came out of energy, and it always provided the satisfaction of having endeavored mightily to create a work of art that deserved to live on its own. In the doing, it wasn't satisfying, it was work, it was taking years of experience of absorption of influences and then struggling against the bristles of the brush or the knife or any other paint-applying tool that was responding to the pressure of my hand and my mind. At the end, when it felt complete, when I could stand back, feel that this was it, that it was done, that's when satisfaction could begin to drape over me and warm me and assure me. The doing of the work was a driving pull, sometimes it just had to be attended to. The pull was strong now, but there was this other matter that kept inserting itself into my mind, and it provided enough drain on the pressure to drive on that I knew I had to deal with it first.

If it had just been the break-in, I probably could put it aside and just shrug. But the two events, the break-in and the odd visitation at the gallery were too much combined to shrug it off. Trouble was, I didn't have much to go on.

After thinking about it for awhile, turning things this way and that, after seeing if clearing my mind would let some flash of insight enter, which only resulted in thinking about food, drink, girls and cars, I finally hit on an action of some kind. I called Detective Ramirez in Miami. He was informed who was calling, and he picked it up. We exchanged pleasantries and spoke.

"Anything new on the Hand matter?"

"Uh, yeah, well, let me think. This week alone has been filled with immigration issues and low-level drug busts, so that matter hasn't been at the top of my 'look into' list. But, since you bring it up, I would like to know what's come up. Give me just a moment, stay on, hang on for a minute."

I heard the phone being laid down on a hard surface, then a humming sort of quiet, with an occasional sound like a muffled word somewhere within the range of the phone, but the words weren't intended for me and had no context. The low hum sound changed just slightly, and I was sure a voice would begin. His did.

"Hey, you there?" he began, without waiting for a reply.

"Yeah, I've got the file, and not much has happened. Hand is a good soldier, or a good captain, don't really know which. We don't think he's the top of this, but he isn't saying anything that leads us anywhere. The other two guys, well, nothin' on them, they haven't shown up again. What did happen is kind of interesting. We had instructions out to the management people at both their locations, obviously we don't have people to sit and watch something down the chain like these guys, but a few days ago, the managers apparently checked in on Barton's place, your number two guy, his condo, they said they felt they needed to make sure there was no running water or other problems, and the whole place was empty, all the furniture and everything was gone. All the clothes in the closets, towels, everything. We had already been through everything, so I'm pretty confident we didn't lose any evidence or anything, but it's kinda strange. No one seems to know anything about it, you know lots of those units are second places for people, so there isn't somebody around all the time. But obviously, some movers or guys with a truck just came and emptied it. So, of course, we got on with the other place and sent the managers to look. It was empty too, only this time some neighbor had seen the guys, the movers, or whatever, but nothing out of the ordinary, combination of our local flavors, black, brown and crème. But there did seem to be a lot of them, like seven guys the neighbor thought, although he couldn't be completely sure. Big, new, nice look-ing enclosed truck, that's all he got on the vehicle. But, maybe, there is one thing. This old guy, you can guess, doesn't have a whole lot else to do, so he keeps watching. Our guys ask him what they're wearing, what they look like, you know the drill. So the old guy does his best, jeans, some shorts, all muscular, t-shirts, then the notes say, he said two of them had a similar-looking emblem he says on the front of the t-shirts. But, they were different, he says. One was a white emblem, the other was red. He described the emblem as looking like a firework going off, a bunch of stars that ended in one big star. Well, it could be several things, but there is a gym in, shall we say, one of the harder parts of town, that uses something you would describe that way as their logo, and of course, you can get it on a t-shirt, in lots of colors. The thing about this gym is that we think it is part of a business group, hell, we don't know, maybe a business empire, maybe a criminal business empire, because we have busted lots of bad guys, and they are often picked up wearing some kind of thing, hat, t-shirt, from this place. We've wondered whether it wasn't a hangout, or maybe a recruiting station, for low-level thugs. But, the point I veered away from, is, there are a number of these, uh, enterprises that we've picked guys up from, and they are wearing this gear. We don't think it's a gang, these guys don't act that way. They just seem to be independent low lifes, and somehow they accumulate there. That's the 'here might be somethin' part. Unfortunately, we haven't had the time or the smoking gun to track this all down, see whether there is organization of some sort here and what all they might be up to."

That was a bunch of information.

"Umm, hmm, gee, maybe this is something I could look into."

"Yeah, I'm so surprised you would say that" he replied.

He continued, "You know that I would like to know more, and that I can't encourage you into this, but, you should also know that, while I describe the guys we have busted, or talked to, as low lifes, there are two important things to know. First, every one of the guys we've encountered is tough, ain't no softies here, and many are gym rat types, lots of muscle, and, not to be stereotyping anyone but not a lot of brains, but that doesn't mean that somewhere there isn't one or more brains. And that gets to the second thing. It just feels like there is someone or something kinda big lurking behind all this, and that person or group of persons is likely to be very mean and very dangerous, and not going to be happy about anybody prodding on them. I know you get this, right?"

"Yes, I hear, thanks."

"The gym is called SlamStar, and here's the address."

I wrote this down.

"You were a big help with Hand and all that. If you decide to poke around this, I suggest, and sorta ask, that you call or leave me a message that you're doing whatever. And that you call back when you reemerge, just so I don't sit around thinking about it. Okay?"

"Very gracious of you, thanks, and yes."

"Anything else?"

"No."

"Okay, gotta go then, ta ta for now.

We hung up.

I started thinking about going back to Miami.

THIRTY

ONCE MORE unto the breach. Thanks, Bill.

You know how you picked up these phrases through your education. Partial quotations from long ago esteemed and eloquent authors. You know a general sense of what they relate to, maybe can name the piece or the author, but that's really it. Every once in awhile there's a guy, and five times more girls, who knows the whole quote, or a lot more of it, or the exact context and what it represents in world history. I'm for that actually, part of the time it can be really interesting. But more of the time, it can be annoying, and it isn't me. I like knowing lots of things, my friends have called me a photographic memory type or have been amazed at how I can recall song lyrics or bands, or, and this is probably the best, that I do try to be well informed and am able to express at least the basic tenets of an issue, but, quoting from memory poems and such, I just don't have it. Although, one of my favorites is 'The moon was a ghostly galleon, tossed upon cloudy seas.' I was up very early one morning, going skiing actually. The moon was up, almost full, and bright as it could be against the dark sky of early morning. There were just a few diaphanous clouds that floated in the moon's influence. I had already been an admirer of the poem's beginning, setting the stage, but when I saw that vista that early morning, that cemented that one for me.

As much as I love the image created through the words and planted into my head by my own visual experience, I have one quibble with it. It has always seemed that thinking differently was an advantage for me. I have always felt that 'tossed upon stormy seas' was a more powerful allusion.

Images aside, I am back in Miami. Checked into my usual place. Got my work necessities together, some water, an apple, some cheese, it wouldn't be as good without a little red wine, but, it is work. Picked up some newspapers from the boxes in front of the hotel, had some magazines as well. I know these things are no longer as popular, there are so many other places to get information. But when you're staked out, if all you do is sit with your phone perched on top of the steering wheel as you stare out, you are more noticeable, and people assume you're a cop more than if it's written material you're perusing. So, I had some diversions to pass the surveillance time, as that was the extent of my plan. I found my spot, on the street, with a view of the entrance to SlamStar. Ramirez was right, the neighborhood was less than savory. On one hand, there wasn't a whole lot of traffic or activity, so there weren't that many passers passing by to wonder why I was just sitting in my car. On the other hand, there wasn't much traffic or activity, so everybody that came by looked at the guy sitting in the car. Not sure what their thought process was. I wasn't at all sure how long this would work.

The edifice was not particularly interesting. The building appeared to be two stories tall and was grey brick for the first floor and grey stucco for the second. Not much for façade interest, no detailing to speak of. The surrounding buildings were each about the same height and equally nondescript. Really eye-catching, here in the home of bright blue skies and tropical colors.I was able to observe the comings and goings, at least of the front entrance to SlamStar. And they were indeed of the gym set. Mostly t-shirts, with arms bulging.

Occasionally a slighter person would come or go, everybody needs exercise, so I didn't make much of that. Primarily it was guys, entering, exiting, but there were some girls too. Some of the girls had muscular definition almost as pronounced as the guys. Some were just very athletic looking. Those always got an extra appreciative look from me. I watched, I wondered. Should I move? Would it look odder to just stay in one place, or to be here then there, then somewhere else? I concluded for myself that staying in one place was the better choice, and then tried to project that as positive thought energy onto the street in order to influence any minds that might be so influenced. Likely anybody noticing it would conclude that I was probably tracking down someone, but I tried to project that I was just a low-level watcher gathering some evidence on a missing person or cheating spouse, and that I should just be ignored by most of those coming and going. I've tried this telepathic approach before, and it is not perfected.

After awhile I found myself antsy. I thought to myself that I used to be better at this. I used to be able to get into a mindset of calm, and just sit and watch and wait. But, I don't know whether it was the neighborhood, or the fact that I didn't have a good focus on what I was watching for or hoping would happen, or just because I wasn't as practiced at this as I once was, that I found myself fiddling, tapping my foot, tapping my finger on the water bottle, annoying myself with both the tapping and the generally antsy-ness. I needed to do something. I decided to walk. I got out of the car and turned and went away from the gym. That'll fool 'em I said to myself. I had the layout of the block and surrounding area, and it seemed like it could be useful to know what the back entrance area might be like, or any other ingress-egress points that the gym building might offer.

I walked. It was good to be doing something other than sitting. So now I was approaching the gym building from another direction. Ah, what clever subterfuge. There was a kind of alley that went from a side street toward the building. I went down it. It didn't seem like a common access alley, there were no doorways or trash cans or such on this paved via. It turned out that this hard paved passageway did serve the back of the gym, and there was a blank door and trash bin, so this was apparently just a service way. So, it seemed reasonable to conclude that clients of the gym wouldn't access the gym this way, but it was an access. Besides the room it would take for a truck to pull in, there was room for maybe two or three cars to park, although there weren't any parked here now. I walked back out the service way, and found more comfort as I approached the street by walking in the center of the paved way, in order to have as much time to react to anything that might be lurking around the corners of either side of the walls lining the alley. For some reason I really was on alert when I got to that point. I looked quickly both ways. Nothing either side. I sighed a little 'hmm', crossed the street and felt more comfortable on the opposite side, looking back up the alley and down the side street each way. I thought to myself, wonder what that was about, am I just nervous? I walked the length of the side street and turned onto the street where the gym entrance was. I could see my car still parked on the street a ways down.

I considered not walking the length of the block in front of the gym entrance, about going around the block, but maybe because I was building my confidence back up after that uneasy feeling at the alley, I made a mental sneer that indicated I was tough and started walking the path that would take me past the gym entrance, albeit on the other side of the street, and back to my car. I walked casually, although I still didn't feel casual. There were two sets of double doors that were the entrance to SlamStar. Both were darkened obscure glass with steel security bars. As I got perpendicular to the first, both sets simultaneously opened and three muscular guys strode deliberately out. And now they are walking toward me. What? Video surveillance? I had tried to subdue the notion that I would be eventually spotted, although maybe my lack of commitment to that notion undermined the hypnotic trance I had put on the street. Well, here they were. Maybe they just wanted tips on better dressing. They could use them.

Being taken captive just wasn't appealing to me. It's not a good move, not good as a career move, not good for the ego, and probably not good for long-term survival not to say anything for a flourishing existence. I had an unusual opportunity in high school. The gym class instructor was much older and clearly old school. He wanted us to have boxing as a part of the curriculum- part of the 'physical experience of learning' he liked to say. Boxing? Nobody in our class, and I doubt anyone left in the school at that time, wanted anything to do with boxing. To his credit, when a couple of the guys, and one girl too, made the argument to him that 'like, you know, boxing is passé', a popular term then, although I was always sure ninety-nine percent of those that used it couldn't spell it, 'but we could do martial arts', he went with it. As I said, to his credit, he adjusted. A very good lesson to observe early in life. So it was that in high school gym class we threw softballs, kicked soccer and kickball balls, threw footballs, ran, did pull-ups and learned at least something about martial arts, which occasionally included exchanging a few punches. I always wondered whether he knew that was going to happen. Good guy, Mr. McClain. He liked boxing, grew up with it, but he recognized it held little interest, other pursuits held more appeal, and he let us have just a bit our way with the more sophisticated appearing pursuit of martial arts, and guess what, a martial arts kick or jab got slightly off the mark and guess what erupted next, some boxing, although only of the unsophisticated style of untrained free swingers. Well, then imagine what would happen. Some instruction on boxing technique would get inserted to show how to brawl more effectively, and everybody learned something new, to them, old to him. For me, it was all kind of fun, and ultimately, extremely useful.

So, here we were, three against one. I was still a bit edgy from my uncertainty in the alley, so perhaps I didn't consider my chances accurately. I started with my version of rope a dope. Arms straight down at my sides, a slump to the shoulders, a look of resignation on my face. The lead guy got to my space and reached out to grab me, saying something on the order of 'hey we want to talk with you'. Then why are you grabbing me? A chacha twirl, it was an interesting move, then leverage using his arm and the lead guy was lurching head-first to the ground. James Bond always fought hard to not be captured. Now I was confronted by guys two and three. I gave the appearance of raising my hands to surrender, and two moved to grab me. I used that little bit of momentum to grab his outstretched arm spin him and propel him into three. These guys were big and strong and probably expected most folk to wither when confronted. I was far quicker but, really, if one of them did get his arms wrapped around me, I could cause his shins and maybe another place or two some pain, but I wasn't grasshopper, so finally, it occurred to me that one of my other attributes, speed, might be best utilized.

Now. Three hadn't expected the sumo butt from two and went down, but two gained his footing and turned back for another go. I was already running. I heard the shot and absorbed the knowledge that the slug hit in the street somewhere close. I dodged between parked cars and down the sidewalk. I heard the next shot and felt the sting across my side in almost the same instant. But I was also in motion. Now the 'where did that come from?' popped up on the screen of my brain. The three were wearing shorts and t-shirts, not a gun rig on any of them. But my brain moved on. Can I get in the car, which is facing the direction I don't want to go, and get turned around and get out of here? I was within reach of the car. I was looking at the driver side, figuring how I was going to do this. I only, at the last instant, saw the figure push off the wall and crash into me like those old Dick Butkus commercials that they occasionally show on ESPN Classic to go along with the old football games. The former great Chicago Bears linebacker shutting the middle down. Stops the leak. Four was another of the muscle club. Despite the fact I was in full flight, he stepped into me and 'down goes Frazier'. I was stunned. I think two joined four and escorted me to the gym. I'm not completely sure. Those little cartoon bluebirds were flying around my head.

I didn't lose consciousness. I think. But it had been a pretty good whack, so I wasn't able to absorb what happened next except from this dazed state. We went into the gym building, past some sort of reception stand, then up some stairs, to an office or a room, I don't recall the details. After awhile, my head was clearing, and I felt a wet, cold spot on my side. My shirt was pulled up just a bit and I found a wet towel with the remnants of ice wrapped inside it against my side. There was just a slight bit of blood on the towel. A muscle man standing just outside the door moved away. Then an elegantly casually dressed man walked into the room. The man was elegant in bearing as well, tall, maybe an inch, no more, taller than myself, slender, with light-dark skin polished with a slight tan. The muscle stopped in the doorway, filling it up.

"Hello, senor artista," said Mr. Casual but elegant.

"Your side is fine, not really even a graze, more like a slight scratch. That is quite lucky, although the use of gunfire was not required and was a poor choice, which has been pointed out."

Yeah, okay, I'm getting this, the haze is mostly gone, and he's right, my side doesn't hurt. And since I agree that shooting at me was a bad choice and somewhat over the top, I must be close to regaining my normal composure. Close.

"I am Luis Guzman. You don't know me, of course. You also don't know that we have come close to meeting before, but I realized that you didn't really know much and that it would be better that we did not meet. But now you have come to me. What do you want?"

Alright, I'd better get my head closer to normal. He had a direct bearing. 'Hey, I'm speaking to you, and I get answers when I speak', his look said. I was back and forth as to whether to go with a hard stare and hard response myself, or go with the slight smile, maybe you don't know what you think you know, mystery look. The slight smile version was more engaging, so I thought that would be more appropriate here. Since I had gotten a head bonk. And a scratch from a bullet. And the muscle filled up the doorway. And I didn't really know what I was doing.

"Oh, when did we almost meet?" was the best opening I was able to come up with, not great admittedly, but now I was speaking, and I felt sure it would get better as we got rolling.

"You'll figure that out." His mystery answer topped my mystery look.

"I am going to be direct with you because I hope that when you have an answer, you will see that you would rather return to your painting and that will be best for all. You stumbled upon three men that did some business for me. That was unfortunate. But that is the end of that. It was a very small operation and means almost nothing to me. And that is all there is to know about that. So, there is nothing more for you to be involved in. Go back to San Isabel and paint. You have a good style and you do well with it. Because if you don't, only those who already own your works will benefit because of the limited number of works that you managed to create, before your untimely death, which of course always increases an artist's value, for awhile."

He smiled at me without warmth.

"Maybe I should buy one or two of your paintings for myself." Then he shook his head and said, "No, no, you're smarter than that."

He turned and walked, the muscle moved into the room clearing the doorway, and he was gone. Gee, I guess that was the end of the discussion. A second muscle man moved into the room and both took an arm each, I stood up, the wet towel fell to the floor, and out we went. The muscle took me out to my car, pushed me against it without any real enthusiasm or commitment to the action, turned, and walked away. Do as you're told. Hmm.

Ah, well, one of my problems. I don't take direction from someone I'm not impressed with too well. Well, basically,

I don't take direction well, and particularly when it comes with someone poking a finger in my chest and telling me what to do. In this case, it was more like a gun poking me in the chest, but that only made me pause for an instant. I drove away but stopped as soon as I figured I was out of sight. If this guy Guzman, Mr. big bad guy is here, maybe I could learn something. I wanted to go back to the backside of the gym, figuring that might be what he used as his entrance. I couldn't drive down the service way, so I parked my car just off it down a few spaces from one of the corners that had spooked me. I turned the corner of the alley entry and walked quickly toward the trash parking area. Yes, that's how I thought of it, I was beginning to be a bit annoyed with all that had just transpired. I got within sight and it wasn't a moment too soon, I'd have missed it in another few seconds. Mr. big bad guy slid into the rear seat of, ta da, guess what, another Mercedes, this one with a gold hue, and the door shut. I wouldn't have known that he was in there except for the timing being just right. I was feeling the forces of the universe turn back in my favor once again. Two of the burlies from the gym got in front. I turned and sprinted back to my car.

Here we go again. There were no quick moves to follow with this tail. They moved, not exactly slowly, but not like they had to be somewhere either. I had an image in my head of Guzman waving absentmindedly to his minions on the sidewalk, but there were few minions or any people on the sidewalk, and nobody seemed to pay much attention. It was just an image, the car windows were all tinted so dark you couldn't see anything inside. I didn't think that was legal.

The traffic wasn't too heavy as we moved out of this seedier part of town, but it increased steadily as we made our way to more affluent sections. The pursuit was so easy that it crossed my mind that it might be deliberate, that they were almost literally stringing me along so the bait could keep up with the shark. I didn't like this image. Maybe this guy saw himself as being so big and tough that he didn't care what was trailing along in his wake.

We continued through the much nicer areas of town. Then we crossed a bridge. We were going to one of the special sections of Miami, on the waterfront, on the bay. Big houses behind big gates and fences. Water views. Sun and sky and water. And there they went. The big Mercedes slowed, then the brake lights, then the turn into a gated driveway. As soon as they turned, I was out of sight, so I just stopped. I calculated to myself the timing of the gate opening, them proceeding through, the gate swinging closed, the car moving out of sight. I drove on, past the gate, and I had it exactly right. No net dropped on top of me. Well, I've got some work ahead of me.

THIRTY-ONE

BACK AT MY lodging I did some researching. I looked up the house Guzman had led me to so I could see its layout on the property. Big house, lots of decks, on the water, nice. I called Hig. When he had been just visiting, we had talked about a Ferrari owners meeting he had attended and about a guy he had met there from the Miami area. The talk had been about many things speedy and, just in conversation, this guy also liked speedboats. Hig thought he seemed a pretty okay guy although Hig said he had a sense that this guy didn't get his money and toys from being a banker, or at least not the old image of a Main Street type of banker anyway, as more and more we find out that a lot of those seeming straight-laced guys are crooks in their own right, as bad or worse as when they associated with Snidley Whiplash. He also said that this guy didn't have any trouble attracting the ladies too. He gave me the contact. I called and left a message, and it wasn't long before I got a call back. Sure, he'd love to meet up with a pal of Hig's, how about tomorrow. I ventured into the wanting to take a boat ride, and was it possible I might be able to hire him for a ride. 'Hire me,' he snorted, but good naturedly. 'Come by tomorrow, we'll go from there' he said.

I arrived at the address I had been given. The layout of the property was different, but the whole thing seemed a lot like the warehouse place that Hand had. Different, but similar-looking neighborhood, all low rise buildings, a mixture of industrial kinds of uses and businesses, not seedy, but not all glass and steel suburban façades either. A minimum of deliberately maintained landscaping. I walked in the door bearing the street address and was inside the warehouse. No office reception set-up.

There were cars here and there, boats of varying degrees of sophistication either on trailers or propped upright in place with jacks or props, there's probably a right word or two for these common boat yard devices, but I don't know what the right word is. I noticed that it was a neat and well-kept interior, no junk lying around. Two guys were in the hull of a boat mounted on its trailer, tinkering with something. One was kind of round, and the other was stooped and slight. When the round one saw me, he just held up his arm and waved a greeting. I walked toward them. They both faced me and the round one gave out a 'hi there how ya doing'. You notice how strangers greet you. Often I am met with suspicious and 'I don't know who you are or why you're here and you shouldn't be here anyway' greetings. This was the opposite. These guys were completely comfortable doing whatever they were doing, and they were welcoming. Nice change of pace. "Hi," I said, "I'm looking for Diego Carbon" ('Car-bone, long o', Hig had instructed me) and left that pause space at the end that said, and are one of you he? But no, they weren't. The slight, stooped one said, 'Oh', and nimbly, unexpectedly nimbly, dropped from the boat hull to the floor saying 'I think he's over here come on'. He said, 'Hi I'm Pete', another indication of openness against the sort I frequently meet who wouldn't tell you their name if they were on fire. 'I'd shake your hand but I've got oil on my hands from fiddling with that engine.' Hey, that's okay.

We found Diego. Right out of GQ. Latin good looks. Athletic profile. Strong handshake. "Hello there, friend of Hig. How is my friend Hig? What, he was in Florida and didn't come to visit? Ah, tsk, tsk, I will have to have a word with him." All with a practically beatific smile, but I did see a hardness in his eyes. I'm gracious, yes indeed, his eyes said, but I am used to being in charge and getting my way. My impression was that he could be a good friend, if your activities didn't challenge his, or that he could be a difficult enemy. We locked eyes for a moment, will we sniff or fight? I think we relaxed simultaneously, at least no fangs were bared. We exchanged some light pleasantries, fellow residents of the sunshine state. Exhibiting grace, he inquired whether I liked 'really fun' cars and would I like to see 'one of' his cars? Hig probably told him I wasn't a member of the club, but could be trusted nevertheless.

I felt for a moment like I feel whenever someone announces that they are a 'Mensa-n'. I have taken the practice test and excelled, maybe I should formally join Mensa just to say 'yeah, so am I, so what?' But the feeling passed, and I said,

'Oh, sure' and we went to one side of the warehouse space, where, it wasn't very noticeable, there were locked door spaces that ran along one portion of one of the walls. It was hard to tell whether it was intentional that the doors to the locked spaces just blended into the adjacent walls, but that is what they did. Diego took a fob from his pocket, a quiet bleep, and the overhead garage type door began to roll up. First I saw the low profile of very black tires and then the body came into view. Red. Pointed. Slung. Exotic. Assemble your own sports car magazine description of a body that makes you want it. Despite the fact I was ready for it and wanted to believe I could say, 'Oh, another Ferrari', the sight was, all right, magnificent. I know a few of the styles. I recognize the Daytona body, the 308GT of Magnum fame, the F430 that I had just had the pleasure of seeing and piloting. I recognized others in that way that you are just certain that 'that's a Ferrari'. But I'm not there with the 'I know every body/engine /chassis/brake pad lining guys, and I've met more than a few girls who are also in that club. I love the way these cars look, I enjoy knowing something of the history and dedication it took to make them rise to their level of public perception, which is based in the reality of performance and looks. But my line is drawn.

It is not necessary for my happy existence to be able to identify the car as some identify blue warblers from pink sapsuckers. Sorry, I have spent some enjoyable moments with a morning cup of coffee watching birds flit about, and I think anyone who wants to have the expertise to know exactly one from the other is to be commended, but it's not me. Ah, well, back from my mind's flight of compensatory rationalization for not owning one. It was magnificent. He introduced it, a 430 Scuderia, one of only some limited number. I have driven hundreds, maybe into a thousand or so, miles in Ferraris, so it's not like I've never touched this particular holy grail and the car he was showing me is a close relative to Hig's car. This was one of the reasons Hig and Diego had hit it off. Hig also told me that he had extended an offer to Diego to come to his track sometime, an offer that is only sparingly given to others. Suddenly Diego was apologetic. 'I know you are very familiar with this and with other performance machines', he said. 'You must forgive me, it is I that gets a little carried away sometimes'. Ah, his Latin grace was pushing to the fore. And maybe an ability to read faces or reactions. 'It is just fun to share this beauty, this emblem of beauty and power, with someone who also appreciates it like I do'. Very astute, now he has made me, at least, an honorary club member. I relented the resistance growing in my own head and was able to sincerely compliment the car for what it was, beautiful in repose, exhilarating in the projection of the image of it in motion. We found a place of peace among the three of us.

THIRTY-TWO

"SO YOU WANT to go for a boat ride? Yes? Let's go." One of the vehicles parked inside was a platinum grey Range Rover. He motioned to get in. Okay, not much in the way of discussion, no 'and why do you want this' or 'where do you want to go?' Just, 'let's go'. This place wasn't on a waterway. It was only minutes to a small marina area, tucked into an industrial waterway section. We exchanged low common denominator small talk on the short drive, weather is nice, sky is clear, we both like warm weather, and fast cars. We stopped close to the dock. He said, 'here we are', we got out and walked to another gleaming embodiment of wealth, power, and beauty. The blue exterior of the cigarette boat was perfect. It blended several hues of blue, and it reflected both the sky and the water. The water here wasn't the beautiful water of the open sea or the bay, but it was easy to infer how this hull would become one with its environment on the open water with the sky flying overhead and the waves rushing beneath. We stepped into the cockpit. The interior had a similar blended hue coloring, with more grays mixed in. It occurred to me that this boat would be much harder to spot in the open ocean than, say a white boat. I wondered whether this was deliberate or merely a reflection of Diego's taste and aesthetic inclination, because the boat did look like it belonged in the water, could be a part of it, could be a large aquatic creature of its own. That was quite an ethereal image to contemplate.

It wasn't until he stepped up to the wheel that he said, 'where would you like to go?' He didn't say, 'I only have an hour', 'I'll have to get fuel', just, without saying it, said, 'I am a man at leisure, and I'm willing to set out on your adventure'. I showed him the map of the shoreline I wanted to traverse, he looked, said 'Ah, okay, I know this'. He went to the bow and released the lines, then went to the stern and did the same, giving a slight push away from the dock, casting us off. He might be a man at leisure, but he also was active and in charge. He could have asked me to do something, but he just did it. The throaty purr when he engaged the engines belied what this aquatic machine could do. I've seen these boats race, and it is both picturesque in how they at times skim the water surface, and brutal in how, despite their ability to blade through the water, the inevitable chop of the surface can make them bang and slam. A long voyage in these, heck, even a short voyage, can drain you, even when you are buckled into padded, shock-absorbing seats. I really did like the burble of the engines though, as we moved away at wakeless speed.

For some reason I felt very different about this than I had about being shown the Scuderia. Maybe I was jealous of the car. But the boat, I really enjoy going out on the water like this, but having somebody else be the one who owns and is responsible for the boat is very okay with me. I wouldn't do it enough to make it worthwhile, and it is a lot of work, and cost, to keep any boat worth having in good maintenance. Yes, going for a ride on someone else's boat was just right. I felt I needed to be complimentary, and, in fact, I wanted to be. Our speed had increased, but it was still a smooth and gentler ride than I knew at some point we would experience. The airflow across us, in the open air, was not yet to the strength where words merely came out of your mouth and were then swept over the stern.

"This is sure beautiful, Diego."

"Yes, thank you, I very much enjoy the free feeling of cruising in this boat, thanks for getting us out."

Boy, gracious as could be, thanking me for this indulgence, without having received the common decency of a complete explanation.

"When we get over there we will go at a nice pace, not too fast, not too slow, juust right," he smiled at his humor. "But we are away from the restrictions now, so let me show you a bit of what she can do."

He told me this, but then looked and said, 'Yes?' Giving me the chance to join in agreement. I smiled, nodded, and said, "Yes." The engine sound increased steadily to roar, and it felt powerful. The water cascaded by as the bow cut through smooth and less smooth portions. The bow only bounced lightly when there was chop, the speedboat showing its pedigree to handle much rougher stuff. It was exhilarating.

Soon we began to slow. Diego gestured with his chin that we were approaching the area I had indicated as being of interest. From two properties away, I could spot the one I was seeking. As we approached the edge of the property, its pedigree was apparent. The grounds rose from the shoreline like an emerald carpet rising out of the blue waters of the bay. The house topped the carpet with white stucco walls and angles and glass and projecting decks with thin tubular horizontal railings. Several of the decks had roof-like coverings of canvas or a more advanced material that were architectural and engineering masterstrokes of cream, glazed earth brown, and black. It was like a colorful sailing schooner of modernistic design moored to the earth. There was no one in evidence, no one lounging on any of the many loungers available. No one sitting in the shade, no one taking advantage of the sun gloriously lighting the angled walls and surrounding terrain. I had another image, the house had the appearance of a palace. We cruised on past and past several other worthy looking places, but they didn't have the same spark or proud bearing.

Diego said, "The big modern white one got most of your attention."

I nodded acknowledgment.

"Shall we go by again?"

"Yes," I said. We did. Nothing visible had changed on the grounds or on the decks. The dock of the property held two boats, both so thoroughly covered that it was hard to tell exactly their type. There were no jolly rogers flying anywhere. As we passed the property boundary, I turned to look at Diego. His eyebrows raised indicating 'what now?' I said,

"Thanks, let's head for home." We didn't change speed until we were several more properties away, and even then Diego increased the speed only gradually, unobtrusively.

We reached the speed-restricted area on the way in, and I took advantage of the quiet engine pulse and slower air movement to confide in Diego what he had been such a good sport about, about my starting point with the drug runners and now about Guzman. And that I had learned nothing, except how well he was living, from the ride. He said it was worthwhile because you need to see these things for yourself, and maybe it will help come up with a plan.

We reached wakeless, and Diego said, "I know a little something about this guy. I've never run across him personally—they refer to him as el sombra, 'the shadow'. He seems to be somewhere behind many different, ahh, activities. There are also stories that he can be a little bit 'hands-on', that he doesn't just have his people doing things, that he likes to be directly involved, to lead the charge sometimes. Maybe it helps him keep track of what his people are doing, maybe he thinks if they see the general in the fight, they will fight harder, or not cross him. But that is about all I think I know."

I nodded. We pulled into the dock, shut the engines down and tied up. This time I held the stern line while Diego tied off the bow. I know a few knots and could have tied it up, but sailors and captains alike each seem to have 'their way' of tying up and I left it for him. On the drive back I politely inquired if I could reimburse him for fuel, or what could I do for all his graciousness. 'No, no, he replied. I haven't been out for a few days and it was good to go, it energizes me.'

Back at the warehouse I thanked him again. His graciousness continued 'It was fun. Good to get out for a little break.' As I turned to leave, he said, 'Don't worry, something will happen, it always does.' I hoped his optimism would be catching.

THIRTY-THREE

MY PHONE RANG. The number was blocked. Wonder what this will be.

"Padrone, como esta. Hey, it's Diego. It was nice to meet a friend of Hig. It didn't seem like you got as much out of the sightseeing tour as maybe you hoped for, eh?"

There were a lot of different language influences in that greeting.

"Thanks, Diego, yes, I didn't have much of a plan starting out, and that hasn't changed."

"Yeah, that's the thing about plans. Sometimes better to go with the flow and see what happens."

I had to chuckle just a little bit.

"I'm not sure I even know where to catch a flow right now to carry me toward something."

"Well, see, that's okay, maybe I can help. I've got some friends heading over, and another boat or two will be coming as well. We're going to go out for a sunset motor, just cruise. Maybe we'll find ourselves going past the house again, give it another look. You're welcome to come along."

A life lesson: when opportunities present themselves, take it. Or take them. Whatever. Jump on board.

"Ha, well sure, that is a nice invitation, thanks, I would like to join you."

Did I feel the formerly stale air surrounding me start to move a little? To flow?

We met at the dock, not the warehouse. When I got there, there were already some very beautiful people standing around. The ladies sported all the colors of the rainbow and more. Tight white jeans, tight white shorts, turquoise, orange, yellow, even an alluring red. Two new boats were tethered together one after the other to Diego's, it seemed all the other moorings at the dock were spoken for, but it made it easy to climb from one to the next. These other boats were not the ultra-long elongated style of Diego's go-fast boat. These were cruisers, more room for partying and hanging out, in fact, with some owners they are called 'walk arounds' because you can do just that on them while on the water. There were coolers standing open, packed with ice, and offering wines, beers and some pretty exotic picnic fare, cheeses and sliced meats and even one filled with shrimp. The party was underway, and I joined in. In a moment Diego was at my elbow. It was hard not to sink to the level of collegiate familiarity.

"Gee, do you think you know how to have fun?" Understatement at it's most lame.

"Well, we do enjoy a good time, and I'm glad you joined us," he raised the level of repartee.

Let's go," he said to me, then "LET'S GO!" he said to the assembly.

It sure was fun to watch the lithe and tightly wrapped carriages bend and lean and step over one gunwale to the next, as everyone apportioned themselves relatively evenly among the boats. They cast off, one after the other, into the early evening spell of sun spilling its low rays onto the glimmering water surface.

Three boats, with gloriously good-looking people, it looked exactly like it mostly was, a sunset cruise, enjoyment of the water and great warm weather.

It was easy with the flotilla to cruise slowly past the house, even to linger because there was more to see on the water than there was on the shore. Once again, there didn't appear to be any activity at the house. Ah, well, the air was moving on the boats and there were other scenic distractions. Every now and then the boats would stop and congregate, exchange passengers. At any viewing from practically any distance, it was clearly a floating party going on. At the best viewing point for the house, we all slowed and congregated once again. Diego had taken occasional brief leaves of absence from the helm but never left his ship and was now captain again. I had moved among the boats having fun chatting with a whole lot of people I didn't know at all and enjoying all the great sights that were on offer. I reboarded Diego's ship and moved up to talk with him.

"Diego, this is great fun, thanks."

"Yes, but there hasn't been much on the other front has there?"

"No, 'fraid not."

"The sun won't be with us for much longer now, so we'll just float for awhile, see if anything is up."

"Okay by me, thanks."

We continued to move, slowly, with the current. The cruising part, in these big powerful boats, is fun. Fun to feel the bit of spray, the rushing air, fun to be out in the great openness and to soak in the feeling of being alive with the accompaniment of the evidence of the vastness that surrounds each one of us. There's a feeling of individual power at the same time as acknowledging the small place we occupy in the universe. Our transports, the boats, move sometimes gracefully over the waves but the ocean is never static, and mostly not smooth. This means that there are bobs and dunks and even the occasional slam of the hull through even a small wave. And that's at slow, cruising speed. When these things get to moving at speeds they are capable of, at times the ride can best be described as jarring.

But we had resumed a comfortable cruising sped. The girls waved back and forth to each other from their different poses on the boats. Scenery worth seeing for its own value. I poured a little more champagne into my glass to enjoy the wind-down knowing that we would soon be heading to port as the sun appeared ready to touch its brilliant edge onto the waiting mass of the land behind us, then allowing darkness to begin to embrace us.

We were on a homeward tack and approaching the last pass by the house. There was something different. There had been two previously covered boats at the properties' shoreline dock. Now one of them had had its cover pulled back, and it was a go-fast boat similar to ours. No one was visible on or alongside the boat, but the only reason to uncover it was to prepare to take it out. I looked toward Diego only to see that he was looking at me. He nodded. I moved alongside him.

"Maybe the current has changed," he said simply.

Maybe.

We continued on past the house and past several of the other compounds lining the shore. Diego summoned the fleet. The boats congregated again, exchanging passengers just as before, the party obviously continuing. But this time, with Diego hugging and kissing each of the female guests and speaking quietly to some of the male ears, we were the only ones remaining on his boat. I had alternatively been appreciatively watching the enticing female shapes bending and lifting and changing positions, as had been a favorite viewing occupation for all the guys all through the party cruise. I had alternated these views with views back to the docked uncovered speedboat. At a point where the sun had halfway penetrated the land, people appeared on the dock and boarded the uncovered speedboat. As the last shapely rear had disembarked to one of our other flotilla boats, the docked boat pulled out into the great vast flow of the darkening ocean. Diego signaled to his lieutenants piloting the other boats and slowly, with great reserve, began to put power to his engines. We left behind the safe embrace of the flotilla, of the party time, and embarked on a solo mission laced with uncertainty.

THIRTY-FOUR

DIEGO PULLED AWAY slowly from the other two boats, which just sat in position. For a short while we would be visually inseparable from the others viewed from afar, but that wouldn't last for long. It was easy to track the other speedboat. They had running lights on and were going at only a steady pace, not breakneck speed. The sun was entombed for the day, sinking behind us, hopefully to rise again tomorrow, but for now, its light was being extinguished. Diego and I had not talked about this pursuit, nor about any strategy that would be involved, but the action of following the speedboat had been without hesitation, we were in the flow, and we were propelled to take this action. It wasn't clear to me what interest Diego had in this or why he would so willingly undertake this pursuit. I stood alongside Diego at the controls. I couldn't pilot this boat as effectively as he could. He was calm and this seemed like a natural environment for him. He didn't close the distance between the just visible focus of our attention, simply following, for now, the trail set by the lead. I looked out, casting my view around, just to do it. It occurred to me that I didn't see a bow light on our steed and from my position to one side of the helm it didn't seem that we had a running light at the stern either. I couldn't see to Diego's stern side, but I felt pretty sure in the realization that the lights didn't show deliberately, not for lack of maintenance. Is this one of my tricks that he knows, or the other way around? The hum of the engines was steady and not overpowering. The air hitting us in the face limited conversation more than the engine throb. I tried anyway.

"Do you think they can see us?" I asked.

"It's getting much harder to tell now," he said, "but I have been watching, and not one of them ever looked around. They seem pretty set on where they're going and either don't expect or don't care, or more likely, think that when the time comes, they will easily outdistance or lose in the darkness any tag-a-longs. It's a little bit of typical cockiness in their actions so far I think."

He didn't say it, but the set of his face and his frame at the wheel said, 'but they don't know they've got me behind them'.

He started again. "I'm expecting that when they decide it's dark enough or at the right place they are going to hit it, and douse the lights. That will make it more difficult, but for now, I have confidence about keeping up. Also, I think I have a sense of, well, if not exactly where they're going, of how they will navigate to get there."

He had not turned his gaze away from the quarry while he spoke this, but at the end he finally did turn and look at me. Even with the darkness surrounding us his smile was that of a confident brigand, relishing the feeling that he was superior and enjoying the chase. His dark eyes, caught by the slightest bit of lunar illumination as the moon made a brief, cloaked appearance, also flickered with a 'this is good times' enjoyment. This guy knew his surroundings, knew his and his boat's capabilities and had a good bead on what to do. Was this just a game for him, a fun diversion from boredom? Yet, he seemed to know this kind of action pretty well. Was there more in it for him than I could perceive? For the moment I was glad he was captain.

His gaze was straight ahead now. "It's been fun" he began, "but I think we'd better get ready for what's next. Get into the chair and get buckled in," he said as he did the same one-handedly, with experienced ease, keeping one hand on the wheel.

I did as he recommended. I saw the lights in the distance blink off.

"Now nobody has lights," I said almost absently, noting the obvious.

Diego turned his head just partly and I could just make out the continuing confident grin on his face.

"I know how to party, eh," he said. "Here we go."

I heard and felt more power being applied to our engines. After a few seconds of this accelerating surge, I heard us pass through the left behind sound pulse of the increase in their engine demand, like passing through thunder when you knew the lightning had occurred brief moments before. This concreted for me what I had realized before, without really thinking about it. We had been headed into the wind, although it was hard for me to know how strong it was because of our own speedy passage through the air. The wind coming at us took our engine sound out beyond our stern and wouldn't be heard until the wind changed or we ran right into them. Neither seemed worth worrying about right now. We are firmly committed to the flow.

We left behind our party group more than an hour and a half ago. We had been going forty to forty-five knots at first, then when they hit and we followed we started going seventy knots. In my rough calculation, although my seasoning as an ocean-going commandant is considerably less than Diego's, we should be close to our point of no return. I was enjoying the ride a bit less now. The pounding through the chop and now waves takes its toll. The wind in our faces had clearly gotten stronger, noticeable even over the rush of our speed. The wind had gotten blustery, so at moments it hit our faces with a force that made us tuck our chins in and duck into it. I was also wondering about fuel. There is great variability with this type of boat, fueled up they generally have a range of around two hundred miles. I could always say to Diego, okay, that's enough. Let's go home. Aside from being an odd thing to suggest at this point, Diego didn't seem to be losing his enthusiasm for the race or the chase or whatever it was we were doing. That could be a part of my unease I realized. I was just a passenger at this point and I don't like being a passenger. I am happier in the captain's chair. I was thinking again that I didn't know why he would so easily embrace this chase. I had only the very slight reference from Diego that he 'knew a little something about this guy'.

Diego was doing a great job, an almost extraordinary job of following something out there that I couldn't see. Since I wasn't doing anything except bracing, trying to relax, brace again, I had time for my mind to wander. Did he have eyes like an owl? I did notice slight course corrections. We were still the beneficiaries of the wind bringing their engine sound to us. I had begun to get the rhythm of it but was certainly behind the curve. When Diego would shift course slightly, I realized the sound had changed, perhaps slightly fainter, then he shifted course and the sound would stabilize, for lack of a better description. I had not figured out how he knew which way to shift, because I didn't hear it. I tried to console myself by saying it was because he was at the helm and therein under the pressure of performing. If I had to be in charge, then you rise to the level of the challenge. I wasn't actually convinced. At any rate, he was a good tracker. Maybe he's done this before. I wondered.

We had benefitted from the wind and from the heavy clouds overhead. With bright moonlight, even if the guys we were following were cocky and didn't much care, there was a higher likelihood of at least a casual look around from one of the boat's occupants, and maybe we would have been spotted. I had contented myself that they were braced against the air beating into their faces as it was ours and they were just focused on where they were going, which could be anywhere as far as I could tell. Now, the heavy cloud cover became less of a cohort. Little drops of water that were coming from the opposite direction of the sea spray became to come at us. It wasn't heavy, but it would add another element to our quest.

Before, when we didn't have to hang on so much, we had gotten some foul weather gear ready at hand, so we were prepared.

We motored on further into uncertainty. The rain got a little heavier. I was thinking I would try another calculation, with my mind's guess being that we were two-thirds of the way through our fuel and what did that mean for survival.

I heard it at the same time Diego did, because it was a one, two reaction. I heard it, and he cut the power, so he heard it at the same time. The whoosh of the rain hitting the water surface and us had made listening for the motor sound even more difficult. When Diego cut the power, we knew we weren't hearing it anymore. We stopped moving forward except to conclude our coast. Diego had the engines as mute as possible, at the lowest possible idle. Conversation wasn't a lot easier with the velocity of the wind continuing to rise, and then, of course, the rain.

"Three choices," he said, "they turned, or they stopped."

I knew that he meant they turned right, or left, or stopped. Three choices.

"I feel like going left because that is not my natural choice, and it certainly feels unnatural out here."

Hard to offer a counter command to that.

He advanced the power steadily. Now all the wind and rain was coming from the side. We both raised a hand pointing ahead at the same time. Was that light? It was almost straight ahead, but not close, and only pinpricks of light made it through the up and down of the waves and the obscuring effect of the rain. Diego did not back the power down. We continued toward our last sighting of, something. Then one beam of stronger illumination could be seen. Still, we continued toward it. We got to a distance where we could see the light shining downward, from what source it was still hard to tell. At the peak of our rise in the waves, I thought I saw the light shining on a boat. I looked at Diego, he nodded, and we both saw it. For the first time since darkness had set in, Diego actually turned his body both ways, looking to port and to starboard. It was the most movement he had made in hours. He cut the motors.

"I think I know what has happened," he said. "The sea is too rough for them to moor against the target, my guess is that it is a trawler of some configuration. They needed the light for the boat to rendezvous. Also, they figure the weather is too bad for air surveillance, so they aren't worried about the light, and," his grin returned, "they do not know about us."

Trawler. Have to take that on faith for the moment.

"I think, I think I think I think," he said as if trying to convince himself he was right, "that we are okay, out of sight. I think the wind and everything will carry us beyond the bow of the trawler. We can't get any closer. They often have very bad long-range weapons on these things."

Without power, and of course, the accompanying noise, we bobbed like an ersatz cork in the ebb and follow of the wind-driven waves. Diego had calculated, or guessed pretty well, not only with the direction of turning but also about how we would drift. With the wind beginning to howl, we did not drift at a slow pace. Probably just as well. We passed the bow of the trawler while the light was still shining on the speedboat. From our closer angle in the drift, the outline of the larger boat did have the configuration of a trawler.

"Can you tell the size of the trawler," I asked.

"Oh, it's at least a hundred footer, you can put lots of things on one that size."

Sounded like something he was familiar with.

We drifted out in front of its bow by quite a ways. We just stood and looked, trying to glean out of the darkness, with one ray of light, whatever we could. We got to a point where most of what we could see was simply black. We looked at one another.

"What do you think this is about?"

Diego replied, "I'm certain it is smuggling of some kind, but, I'm wondering if it is drugs. Your guy has gone to a lot of trouble and risk tonight, and it seems to me that drugs wouldn't be worth that. It could be, of course, it could be enough for Miami for a whole, well I was going to say year, but I think they need a bigger boat."

He laughed at this own joke.

"I think it is important, maybe drugs, but," he gave a shrug, "maybe it is something bigger, maybe guns."

We both contemplated that for a moment.

"I have to tell you something," he said.

This could certainly be interesting.

"The weather is getting quite bad. I know something about the weather here on the water. We are a long way from home and even with the wind at our back there are many things that could go wrong in an open boat, even this one. We are not far from, ah, a place we could go and wait out the storm. Ah, we'll have to go into the wind for just a bit longer, but I think it will be better to do that."

I was direct. "You have shown you know what you're doing out here. I vote for your plan." As if my vote would count for anything out here.

He smiled broadly. "Good, you'll like this."

"Okay, so where are we going?"

If possible, his smile broadened. "Cuba."

THIRTY-FIVE

WE STOOD and waited. We had drifted past the bow of the trawler. Would it matter now if we engaged the engines and they heard us? We had no lights. It would take an extraordinary effort to harm us. Still, it seemed contrary to all we had done to just say ha ha catch us if you can. To do that seemed as if it would be an affront to the, what, karma, spirituality, powers of the sea, maybe the whole universe, that allowed us to get this far. And we weren't home safe yet by a long stretch. After a period of waiting, with the rain now pelting and the wind determined to push us somewhere, maybe to the edge of the seas that ancient navigators feared, the place where 'there be dragons', Diego looked at me, and for this occasion, said 'I think now is okay, you", with the unspoken question mark. 'Yes'. The powerful engines burbled to life. He increased power, and we became a dark hull moving through the elements, air and water, wind and rain. It was anyone's guess how long to wait to go full bore. I felt he measured it well.

On the deck of the trawler, gazing out into nothingness, Luis Guzman was pleased that he had weathered the storm and the difficult conveyance. This cargo was very important. He had shown himself, once again, to be the general on the battlefield, unafraid to do the hard work. He was very wealthy, but this new venture in criminal activity would start a new line, one that could be more profitable in a single shipment than a year of drug running. The world was in a difficult place right now, and there were very unhappy people out there who believed that power was in gunpowder. A very old notion, he thought philosophically to himself. And yet, for some reason today there is more money afloat and willing to pay exorbitant amounts for these wares than he had ever imagined. And so he set out to make his place at this table. Not one to think small, he was thinking of ways to make it his table. For him alone.

And then a sound. A powerful sound from beyond the trawler's bow. Guzman quickly retraced to himself the actions of his speedboat trip. When they had reached the meeting position, the trawler was just arriving too, traveling from the south. Because of the roughness of the seas, he and his speedboat crew had transferred to the larger ship. Now the trawler captain was turning the ship about to have its bow headed into the driving wind. They would ride out this storm for as long as possible on board the trawler, but he could not remain on board when daylight came. If the storm did not abate, he might be forced to take refuge on land until conditions allowed him to return to Miami, while the ship continued with its disguised cargo. It was in the trawler's turning that he heard the sound. Like engines. But there were no lights. No conventional craft would be out here without its lights. What else could that be? He strained to listen for more, heard nothing, then heard just one more stanza of engine power before a big wave crashed into the not yet well-positioned bow, and sea spray and rain combined to douse the deck as if in a waterfall. Time to go below and wait it out, he concluded, with unanswered questions resting uneasily in his mind.

We had waited as long as seemed right. Diego didn't put the power to the engines all in one moment, like some teenager trying to impress all the bystanders with his noise. He did push it forward steadily, and, at a point, well, it was time to scream. The optimum efficiency in these boats is often reached at a very high speed, not their maximum speed, but at their rated cruising speed, where speed and fuel efficiency were at their balance. The optimum cruising speed for this beauty was about eighty knots, ninety miles per hour. The heavy seas took away some of that efficiency. The heavy seas made the battering we took worse. The thought of being out of the water, from both below and above, was a goal to reach for. It didn't take twenty minutes to put the goal in reach.

Diego eased off the power. The engine rumble quieted to a murmur. Diego was sizing up the situation.

"We are close now. We must do what we can to keep our eyes and ears aware. It is not typical for any patrol boats to be going without lights, they would rather that their presence be known so as to be a warning, also that way they don't have to work too hard. On top of that, you have the weather. They aren't patrolling to prevent a foreign attack, they don't have anything to take. It is more to keep the people in check, and to put up a show, a very uncommitted show of deterrence, to smuggling. Most likely the patrol boats don't want to be out in this bad weather, they can report that they were protecting their men and equipment, the kind of excuse that makes sense when you don't have a commitment to being the best. But…" he drew this out, "if you have lived life," he looked directly at me, "and I expect you have, there's always a zealot somewhere, and you had best be prepared for that."

I agree with him. Having things to strive for in life, having goals or having the drive to say I do want to be the best, and then putting the effort to work toward that distinguishes societies that achieve from those who do not. It's not that the people are different, it is the control or attitude that more or less pervades a society whether you can be rewarded for achieving or if achieving only means that all your neighbors get to benefit from your individual effort, mostly then the individual loses the desire to forge ahead. The particular setting we were in offered some different challenges from the conditions that I might more typically get myself into, but the response needed from eyes ears and brain were not unusual for me. Without him suggesting it, I was also already on alert. The rain and wind had not abated. Our landing was to be at a small enclave on the edge of a larger, but still a very small town. Diego was matter-of-fact that we would be fine once landed, but the possibility for trouble was between here and there. The wind that had protected our position by sweeping our sound away, but had required payment in the form of us literally taking it on the chin, was offering both a hand and a slap again. The wind-driven rain in our faces had become our normal condition. The wind was blowing offshore, so there weren't shore-breaking waves to contend with. We came in off the ocean to only the slightest indentation of the shore; it wasn't a bay, just a transition between open sea and land. There were only a few distant lights on shore, and none at the point where Diego was aiming the prow. At only about three hundred feet out, a structure in the water could be distinguished, barely. This was our target. Diego had the engines going so low that they were barely noticeable over the pelting rain and wind. This was also the plan. Now almost to the structure, there were several blank, dark parts that rose from the water. I was struggling to figure out what they were. With a slight turn and at plodding speed, Diego heading into one of the dark spots. I knew it wasn't a black hole and that we wouldn't be swallowed up never to be released, at least until another big bang. It did have the appearance of a tunnel, however. The prow went inside, and it was revealed, it was a fully enclosed, well, boathouse, although it was more of a boat shack. No reason to be derogatory, this was obviously quite functional. The speedboat fit in nicely, with bumpers along both sides that nestled it comfortably. He had gone to full stop on the engines just after the prow had been fully enclosed, he snugged the boat in completely, then came over to my side and took the line that was conveniently hanging there and tied it to the grab bar that had been of great use to me.

Almost as if he were talking to himself and not to me he said, "It's not how I like to tie up, but it has its uses in this circumstance."

Then he nimbly moved to the stern, stood on top of the engine enclosure, reached up and released a rolled covering attached to the roof of the boat shack, which dropped down to conceal the stern of the boat. He tied it at both sides and then moved forward to the cockpit.

"Okay, that will do for now."

Above where the line was tethered, he reached for and found a latch, released it, and a partial door swung away from us.

"After you," he said and made the palm up, here you go gesture.

I climbed out of our valiant chariot, through the adequate door opening, and put my feet down on wood, wood planks to be exact, wood planks of the dock. He followed and then closed the door. I didn't see a latch on this side, but it was dark and the side of the boat shack only partially sheltered us from the wind and rain. I followed him toward shore and beyond the end of the enclosure, where we were once again fully exposed to the elements. But we were on land, or on a dock that would soon put us on land. We left the wet wood of the dock and strode across the wet ground toward a different assemblage of dark structures.

Diego reached into his pocket and appeared to point something small at a building. With a click, a dark door opened and Diego stepped inside first, and I followed. The door closed behind us and a low light came on. There were several men and women inside and a rush of voices greeted Diego. 'Diego estás bien, qué está pasando?' Diego was replying to all at once, 'si, si, si, todo está bien, bien'. I wish I were better at it, and I have made an effort to learn some Spanish, and some French, a bit of Italian, some words in German. Chinese and Arabic, while they would be valuable, have so far escaped me. These simple greetings and questions were easily understood. 'Diego, are you okay, what's going on.' 'All is well' is the general response. And it was.

Diego gave a general introduction of me, in Spanish. I followed it. This was followed by the equivalent of 'I'll explain everything in a moment, but what do you have for two cold, wet voyagers?' A chorus of 'si, si's,' and we were ushered into a small kitchen and seating area. They either had known we were coming or our arrival was well timed with a fresh pot of coffee still bubbling on the stovetop. As one of the women took the pot off, another put mugs down on the well-worn wooden tabletop. Out of the dim light, one of the men delivered a two-thirds full bottle of something, a clear liquid, no label on the bottle, then poured some into four of the mugs before looking around and asking the Spanish equivalent of 'who else?' The woman bringing the coffee poured it into the mugs, two of the men sat down with us. Diego picked his up, as did everyone else, 'todo es bueno, vamos a tomar una copa, salud,' and everyone drank. It was warm, and it felt really good. After the first drink the questions began again and Diego unhurriedly filled them in. It went something like this.

'We,' he gestured at me, 'were out in my boat, look-ing into something. We weren't sure what was going to happen. The people we were watching, one hombre in particular, started off in their boat, and we followed. And we ended up here.'

That was met with a few hoots and the equivalent of, 'Oh come on, what kind of story is that.'

"Es verdad, es cierto" Diego implored, obviously enjoying the outrageousness of this brief telling.

Now began another brief telling of the weather elements, ending with a finger wagging across the table and an increase in suspense that had most mugs on the table and the assembled folk waiting for the shoe to fall.

"Él es un traficante de" he delivered the revelation about the particular hombre, Guzman.

This was met with everything from 'oh my's' and 'how about that's' to versions of 'what, you didn't figure that out?'

It seemed Diego felt it was important to his amigos to be more detailed about this part of the story, and he relayed the look of the trawler, what he had noted as the position and what they all should be aware of and thinking about in connection to the clandestine activity.

While he was telling the stories, I had enjoyed sipping from my mug. The mug was older, all of them were, like something you'd get at somebody's grandmother's house. Nothing wrong with that, it's just what I noticed. The coffee was black and heavier than I was used to, with some hint of spice in it. Very good, just a different coffee version than 'americain' coffee. The additive must have been rum. With the warmth of the coffee soothing away the cold and wet and with the bit of spice and the rum, it was quite nice.

The question got around to 'are you hungry Diego', and 'usted', are you plural 'hungry?'. I wasn't, neither was he. Tired was what was setting in. We were now sheltered, warmed, and in what felt like a protected environment. There were still lots of questions, not the least for me being who are these people, and why are we safe? But that could wait, that will have to wait, for mañana.

THIRTY-SIX

THE RAIN CONTINUED unabated, seemingly, all night. I wasn't awake all night, so I can't say that for sure. I slept quite well. Did wake up once or twice, thought I could hear rain, then adjourned from weather watching and returned to sleeping. It was raining in the morning, that I know to be true. Our hosts had gotten out small, rolled mattresses and some dense blankets that were very similar to woven blankets of the Southwest US. It was like camping—when camping goes absolutely right. The mattresses were comfortable, if not elegant nor wide. I'm pretty sure I rolled off mine onto the floor at one point at least. The blankets provided plenty of warmth. I awoke refreshed, not sore anywhere from sleeping on, or, well, slightly raised from, the floor. This was the house of one of our greeters. The others gathered had withdrawn to their own houses. They were all part of a small enclave, and obviously, Diego had a very strong connection.

Coffee was already ready, or nearing ready. I could smell it. Again, this was like a great camping trip. Now that I'm awake, I can distinguish that this is better than camping, don't have to go outside in the rain to try to start a fire, and then hope the coffee perks right. We were inside, it was dry, and the smell of coffee infused the inside of the house with a spirit of enthusiasm for the day and the tasks ahead.

We had each been given, without requesting, dry t-shirts, by our host, and in handing them out, said to me 'tu los seco', 'to be dry'. He smiled and nodded to my 'gracias'. It was well worn but comfortable and clean. They were very gracious hosts and didn't seem to take it as at all unusual to put up drop-ins out of the middle of a tropical storm in the middle of the night. I kept the t-shirt on and pulled on my shorts. Yes, shorts, this did start off as a sunset-celebrating-good-time-on-the-water evening. My other choice was foul-weather gear.

Diego was already seated at the small wooden table we had gathered around last night, with a mug in hand. The coffee was ready. I picked up a mug from beside the sink, they were on a drying rack so evidently had already been washed, and poured myself some coffee, then lifted the pot toward Diego in the 'how about you?' format. He shook his head and said, "I'm good."

I sat down, looked him in the eye, then read what it said on his borrowed t-shirt, and laughed. He looked down, and smiled. "Good for you," is all he said.

"One question," I said, "I realize the circumstances, but I'm going to ask anyway, uh, I like milk in my coffee, but I'm just asking, I really don't know whether that's appropriate to ask or what, so that's why I'm asking you."

He chuckled, "Don't worry. Café au lait you want, actually me too. It would be café con leche here. Larissa will bring the warm milk when the Cuban bread is ready, that's how they like to do it. I know you know that things are different here, and it's both simpler here and much more difficult. It's always a funny reminder. I'll get by with this black, energized Caribbean coffee, and even with the heated milk in it, it will be a little different than the way I'm used to starting the day. We get used to our own pattern. I really do want to start my day with my coffee with milk, heated milk for that matter, so even I'm not used to this, ah, higher octane, coffee." He concluded with both hands slightly raised in a shrug, and a smile.

I sipped some of the hot coffee. It was good. It worked fine at night with rum. Habit made me wish for some milk. I might drink less coffee this way it occurred to me.

"We'll get some food soon," Diego said, "I really wasn't hungry last night, but I'm ready now."

"Do you want to fill me in on any of this? I like to be a good guest, contribute my share, but clearly, I don't know the lay of the land here."

"Don't worry, we're not putting any burden on Miguel and Larissa, nor any of the others." He chuckled. "You have been a very good guest so far, yes, very good. I also can tell that you know more than a little Spanish. I could tell that you followed most if not all that was said last night. That too rates a good for you."

"Yes, I try to learn more all the time. I think I followed along well enough last night."

Larissa joined us in the kitchen area, saying 'Buenos dias' to me; she must have greeted Diego earlier. I returned the greeting. She smiled. She spoke to Diego, saying that she had some bread, traditional Cuban bread, almost ready, and also moros y cristianos. Great Cuban bread is made all over Miami, but this could be a real treat. Diego thanked her and said 'si, bien'. She turned to her preparations. I wondered to myself what her technique might be to make the seam.

"You know what she said?"

"Yes, she said the bread was almost ready and also rice and beans. Sounds great."

"Oh, good, you have international tastes, that is very good."

I smiled an acknowledgment of his complimentary message, that I wasn't an idiot who wanted pancakes and bacon and eggs in this setting, and that a common Caribbean breakfast dish that had sustenance and nutrition was palatable for me. Yes, I have been arrrounahahndd the world.

Larissa prepared, and Diego talked.

"Well, let's see, to kinda start from the beginning, well, no, I'll just start somewhere. We decided the right thing, the safe thing with the bad seas, was to come ashore. I have on the boat an electronic signal that alerts my, ah, friends, here, that I am in range. In fact, you see that old radio over there, that looks like Pit is just old and probably doesn't work too well? Well, it is the receiver, and it starts playing music when I signal it. It is the only time it plays music. So Miguel heard it start, and it was a surprise of course, but then he got the others, and they waited. All the houses were dark to make it as easy as possible for me, for us, to get ashore unnoticed. So, then, my, ah, friends, here... My parents were from this area, and most of these people are the children of friends of my parents, and there are, I think three of the older generation are still here. Also, two of my crew have relatives here. They like it here, they don't want to go to the States and leave so much of what is natural to them behind, including some family, friends and, well, their heritage. They pretty much get what life is like in the US, but, you know, that is not what everybody in the world wants. I think many more people want to find their way in the surroundings that they feel fit them, where they grew up, where they have their own life memories and their own ties to their culture. Now, everybody in our little group here knows the government is, well, not what anyone would hope for. But everyone here works, so they do okay that way. This is not a crowded part of the country, so there is room to grow some things to go with what supplies are rationed and can be gotten. And there is living in the tropics, it is in most of their beings, they don't want to have it any other way. Plus, there are some benefits we are able to share in return for being a, a, haven. Oh well, you're a smart guy, there's no sense in me... I know a little more about Guzman then I've said, because we, ah, sometimes, not everything, we pursue some of the same, uh, businesses."

Yeah, like I hadn't figured. Except for his knowing more about Guzman. But that wasn't anything to floor me either.

"Okay," he began again, "I was thinking I would tell you we, uh provide transport for smuggled cigars, we do that, and occasionally for someone who needs quiet passage, we do that too, but, ah, well, ah, I do the bad things too, mostly drugs and cash smuggling. Guzman is Mexican, part of one of their cartels. They are very bad people. You have figured this out—I am Cuban-American. There is, a, let's say, rivalry, between our cultures. We think this area is our territory, we don't like the, ah, competition, and we really don't like the way the cartel people conduct business. So, there it is. You know, it's kind of funny explaining this to you. In my world I do what I want and, uh, well, I think I have a reputation as being pretty tough, but I've been going at this like I was telling my grandmother, and feeling bad about telling her. Something I never had to do, of course, but it has left me feeling just a little funny. I haven't figured out why."

Well, that was a relatively complete picture. Sure, details could be filled in here and there, but, well, to ask questions it would come off as, tell me more about your business and give me information that is really none of my business, or, it would come off as almost a groupie panting to know more, because, in truth, I love finding out about the inner workings of any business. Neither seemed the way to go.

Keep it simple. "Thanks for telling me, Diego. It was either that, or you were a secret agent." I was trying to keep it light, but the secret agent part sounded a little stupid as it came out. I needed to recover. "You did a great job, we learned something, maybe you've got a better idea of what to do with what we saw than I do, but, well, I know more now, and that's thanks to you."

The hardness that had been creeping into his face went away and he smiled. "Yes, I'm not quite sure what to do about that either. So you can see that this was an opportunity for me to see first hand what Guzman was up to, and maybe learn something worthwhile to fight him. I'm happy to know what we saw, I'm not sure what to do about it, but…" he trailed off.

"Diego, my story isn't as interesting as yours, and…" I trailed off too. I really was searching for something, anything to say that would be right. It was too sophomoric to say, 'well, I bend the rules sometimes too', or, 'I have an affinity for the darker side, although I haven't acted on it in the way you have', or, 'I'm not a cop, so it doesn't affect me'. None of this was right. In fact, I really was against drug smuggling. Smuggling money, probably the proceeds of drug smuggling, was going to be hard to reconcile, although in Florida there is lots of money that comes there to escape being confiscated from many less stable places in the world. I didn't care about that kind of money being moved around surreptitiously. I would have to care about the drug money because that really was just the same as drugs themselves. Smuggling cigars and people I really didn't care about at all. I liked Diego. This was a bit of a battle going on in my head. I shouldn't like him if he is a drug smuggler. But right now, I do like him. I am, am I, being a hypocrite? The only thing good about this was that this had been going through my head since I first met him, so it didn't take up any time to think this through at this point in our conversation. I didn't know what the ending was going to be, but for now I needed something to say.

"I, uh…"

Larissa came to the rescue. She set down two plates of the steaming hot moros y cristianos topped with a sofrito sauce—onions, green peppers, and spices—in front of us, with a freshly peeled plantain on the side of the plate. She placed the bread on a plate in the center. We both looked up and gave her our appreciation. She went a few steps and called 'Miguel', then came back, got two more plates and put them down. Miguel joined us, as did Larissa. I watched as the three experienced ones each took a piece of the bread that had been sliced in long portions, buttered, then toasted on a grill, and dipped it into their café. I followed suit. Not the normal use of Cuban bread in my experience but I was with natives. The scent of the fresh bread took my head to the best-bakery-in-a-small-town-in-France made bread. We had a wonderful Cubano breakfast.

Not much was said as we ate. It appeared we were all a little hungry. There was a little Spanish back and forth between Miguel and Diego. It was about the rain, and did he know what he was going to do yet. 'No' is a pretty understandable word. We finished pretty much simultaneously, and all said thanks to Larissa. Larissa picked up her plate and then Miguel's. Miguel rose and then so did Diego, giving me the raised index finger of 'give me a moment'. I picked up my plate and Diego's and took the two steps toward Larissa at the sink. She gave me a wide smile when I asked in Spanish if I could help, then shook her head saying 'no, no, no' and shooed me away.

Diego reappeared. "Miguel has been listening for the weather report. The forecast is for this to blow through by midday, and there is nothing else brewing up, at least that they are reporting. That means that the way back to Miami should be okay too. We'll have to make it another night journey of course, because it is just too much a roll of the dice to try to head out in daylight."

That means we'd be leaving tonight. "Diego, I know this varies, but I thought the cigarette boats had about a two hundred mile range. Haven't we used that up?"

"Oh, look at you. The things you know. That's very good. Yes, you are right, the normal range is around two hundred miles. But, when you want certain things in your set-up, you get them. My boat has extra tank space. Getting fuel is very difficult for the people that live here. Imagine me pulling up to where the little fishing boats go and saying 'fill 'er up!' Ha! That would almost be worth it to see the reactions. Ah, maybe someday. But not today. My range is more than three hundred miles, and I can get more if the wind and the seas are right. And, if I don't have to do too much, ah, evasive action. I have been chased by the government patrol boats. Mostly they aren't like the coast guard. Less dedication. You know the coast guard went out and got their own go-fast boats, and they know how to use them. Anyway, most of the local patrols I will blow away even if they do see me, but I still want to avoid that. But back to your question, we should be able to get away and get close to home without too much trouble, yikes, knock on wood! We will send word when we're out there, and my crew will meet us along the way with enough fuel to finish the trip."

Looks like we got ourselves a plan.

We went about the rest of the morning in waiting mode. Cleaned up our bedrolls, listening to the rain, which did seem to be getting lighter and lighter. It stopped around noon. An hour later, the sky was clearing, and the sun made its first appearance. Then it felt like we were in a steam room.

I sat outside, on a weathered wooden bench. The cool air that had been a part of the storm system had been replaced by growing heat. Good thing I like it hot. It seemed like the departed storm had taken not only the rain along with it, but all air movement as well. But there was nothing for me to do, except breathe in and out, and think. Diego came by and saved me from having to do more of that.

"It has been a little more than two years since the last time I went into the little town over there," he gestured to the distance. "It won't be too busy, so I was wondering how you felt about going there."

"It would be great to go. I guess you wouldn't be suggesting it if you didn't think it would be safe for us to do."

"Yes, I think it will be fine, just don't talk too much." He pointed at me and laughed.

We would take Miguel's truck, like everything I had seen so far, an old, much weathered '42 Ford pickup. One of the other men, Pedro, would be coming with us. Strength in numbers. That worked out as far as I was concerned. Three in the seat of the truck, which is far narrower than today's versions, would have been cramped and even dangerous, that is, to the knees or shins of whoever got the short straw and had to sit in the middle straddling the large, old floor-mounted gearshift. A long time ago, I had a girlfriend who had an old car, similar in age to this truck. I don't remember exactly the make anymore, but it too had a tall, floor-mounted gearshift. I do still remember that, when I would occasionally drive it, and she would sit close to me, and I had to shift, it was pretty easy to move my hand from the shifter to her knee, to her warm, lovely thigh, ah, well, nice memory.

So, at any rate, I had already been planning to sit in the bed of the pick-up, the better to observe and take in the scenery. Old joke: Why do cowboy hats roll up on the sides? So you can fit three (or four) cowboys in the front seat of a pick-up. We gathered several of the rug consistency blankets to pad, literally, our seats. Diego and I were each presented with ball caps and coached on bringing the bill down as much as possible to make us less distinguishable. All fine. We set out for town. The truck ran well for its age. There was no need and perhaps a limited ability to go fast, but the steady hum of the engine was confident. Miguel was a skilled mechanic, a handy skill to have here. Parts were usually the difficulty in keeping things going, but he had a supply chain with a long reach, one of the benefits exchanged. The partly sand ground of the enclave was moist and soft, but passable. The road to town was, or had been at one time, a paved road. It still had sections of pavement, but it also had sections that had deteriorated to more of a gravel surface, formed from the disintegrating original pavement. Potholes were rampant, so that too made any ability for speed non-utilizable. We occasionally came to a low spot with standing water after all the rain, but the way was known, as would be expected of an oft-traveled conveyance, and despite the fact I could not see the road surface nor had any notion about the depth of the water at these low spots, Miguel easily took the side where he knew it would be okay and on we went. I was thoroughly enjoying the scenery around us. The dense green of the often-encroaching foliage, trees, and large bushes with very large leaves. Spotted throughout were beautiful dashes of color, yellow orange, red, white, and blue. I chuckled to myself when I saw those last three colors grouped together. In spite of how politicos might wish it, you could find the adopted color representation of probably any nationality in the free growing and blooming botanical world living together in harmony. What a model.

I've bounced around in four-wheel-drive vehicles in the Rocky Mountains. While this road was not that rugged, the same sort of principle seemed to hold for me. The driver, who is holding onto the steering wheel and is thus braced, and who also is in control, picking the path and speed, has the best ride. Everybody else is subject to the bouncing, with less to hold onto and no opportunity for path choice. Despite the bouncing, I really loved being in the back of the truck and absorbed every bit of the beauty around me that I could. I was glad though when it was apparent that we were reaching the town. More and more houses started to appear, most set back a little from the road and noticeable through some amount of screening of roadside green growth. Even though everything was old and weathered, there're few other ways to describe it—that's how everything looks—there were also some wonderful tastes of personality, of vibrant life, of setting oneself or one's homestead apart. There would be a door painted orange. I saw the eaves of one home painted with a light purple, standing out from the grey-brown of the bulk image of the home. Red was a popular accent. Seeing these statements of personality reinforced what we know to be true, people are similar everywhere. For the most part, we bear up under the conditions in which we find ourselves and are familiar to us, but we try to distinguish ourselves in ways that are also comfortable for us. We add some color—we let our personality run a bit. It's worldwide.

The main road did not go through the center of the town. We turned off the main road but were almost immediately in the town. The sights captured me. The town was small, the streets were paved with the same materials as and in the same condition as the main road. That didn't detract one bit. The first view of the town, looking down the main street, lined with small buildings weathered to the color that we associate with bleached bones in the desert, with the dashes and dabs and swatches of colors that highlight here and there, made me feel like I wanted to stay here for a month and paint. I could stand right here, plein air, and see, oh, I don't know, at least a dozen separate compositions that would be rewarding to create and that would grace any wall. The street ran off to the near distance, the sky overhead gradually turned from brilliant blue to a hazy blue green as it extended into the ocean, not far distant but not in sight.

This is living—this is art. My passion for feeling this, for wanting to inhabit it, is what I tried to translate to canvas every time I set out with paint. I was almost breathtaken, grasping the top of the sidewall of the truck, engrossed. The images were flashing in front of me, weathered grey, shaded white, the lightest touch of browns that tried mightily to adhere to wood that didn't mind if the sun and wind and rain banished them from their tenuous foothold on the wood's grain. There is a combination here that stands out from the rest, and it is repeated again and again. It has the background of that hazy blue sky, not brilliant, more soft and welcoming like the sheets on your familiar welcoming bed. Bring forward the light browns turning into the weathered grey. Add some dark brown, the magnificent chocolate of peoples' skin and the unbleached wood that is the tree trunk sheltered by its canopy. Then add a touch of bleached white, and now, set ablaze across it with the orange that somehow holds both red and yellow in its grasp, but yields its blend to the eye. I am totally entranced. Next, I frame an old man's white shirt against the ubiquitous weathered backdrop, set off this time by his faded red bandana. I think of Winslow Homer's return trip to the Bahamas in 1898, particularly his painting 'The Wall, Nassau'. I am seeing all the elements of his work, right here, living and breathing, in front of me. In that painting he captured the expanse of sky over sea in light blues and cloudy whites with the focus in the foreground of a weather beaten, even scarred, wall, then the accent of the red flowering poinsettia rises above the wall, captured in the clear light and atmosphere that I am seeing today. We make a turn and the next image, foreshortened at the corner, is of vertical stripes of white, green, yellow, blue, soft clay reds of the earth and adobe. Oh to capture that instant in the turn. As we square ourselves in the street, the colors spread out, marking that doorway, setting aside this building and then the next, all the way to the next corner.

We turned into an alleyway, found a wide spot, stopped and clambered out, me still in a daze of color and composition immersion.

"Time for something to eat," Diego said. "I want you to try the hamburger." We're in Cuba and what you want is a hamburger? I said aloud only in my head,

We walked around the corner and into a small café. The smell of good things was lingering outside and greeted us before the entranceway. I picked out spices, and smoke and grilled food, and things that I didn't know, but that had a strong attraction. There weren't a lot of tables, what tables there were were small and round, and we moved to one in the corner and took a straight back wooden chair from the closest table, leaving it with just one chair, but adding to the three already in place. They maneuvered me into the corner. The better to be just that amount removed from the server, I guess. Diego spoke to me in Spanish, at the same time as pointing to an item on the small, handwritten menu that felt like it was a combination of cardboard and banana leaf. Could be that was just from use and reuse. A pleasant-looking woman started for our table, and Miguel spoke clearly, 'Quattro bucanero por favor'. He announced that we were four buccaneers? Seemed odd. I was quite content to let it play out, figuring I would eventually find out. She came back with four bottles of beer. Bucanero it said on the label. Now for food. Diego began, asking for 'frita por favor'. She looked at me.

I modified it just a little so as not to sound repetitive. "Quisiera la frita, por favor." It wasn't much, and if she detected the likely North American inflection on the Spanish words, she didn't signal it. The other two made it unanimous. This is the place for frita, and we're going to have it.

Two other tables had two men apiece at them, but they were closer to what was probably the bar area, although it was probably the kitchen's food order-up area as well. There was a soft music coming from somewhere, so we, or three of we, felt comfortable talking low. Miguel asked Diego if he felt confident about the timing of the incoming tide. It would be right about sunset and we would have to go just before, so the risks had to be weighed about starting out while it was still light or having to run the cigarette through incoming waves. Waves weren't a problem when the go-fast boats were motoring under power and had their momentum going, but we had to start off heading out into the ocean very, very slowly so as not to attract attention to the powerful boat that would surely come if the guttural rumble of its mighty engines were even partly engaged too close in.

Diego was confident all would be okay, but that all the men needed to be around to provide as many lookout eyes as possible, scanning for trouble. 'Si, si, sin duda' (of course), was replied. Then it was time to eat. Our server brought plates, each one laden with a fragrant smelling beef patty partly enclosed with what looked to be a homemade, or at least not mass produced, bun. The bun turned out to be made of Cuban bread, unique in its flavor, I had learned after breakfast, with extra moisture part of the mix, and from being made with lard. Ah, this is a very different hamburger. The patty had paprika and onions infused within and came from the grill with a sauce on top that smelled of garlic, and spices, and a touch of citrus. I learned that this is Cuban mojo sauce, an accompaniment with many dishes. Finally, she set in the center of the table, served family style, a plate of thin pommes frites. Potatoes and other root vegetables are a staple in Cuban food, but I didn't know whether french fries were a leftover French contribution or whether it would be claimed as a local heritage - an obvious way to enjoy potatoes. Doesn't matter, didn't matter, it made for a wonderful lunch. The 'hamburger' Cubano style, was fabulous. When we had finished, we all sat grinning at each other for a few moments. I think they were grinning at me because they were pleased that I obviously enjoyed their cuisine. I sat grinning because I very much enjoyed their cuisine. But with the pleasure of lunch concluded, Miguel arose and went to the bar area and paid, probably to lessen any potential interaction with his two foreign guests, one less foreign than the other, and to allow us to hasten on our way. We retook our places in the truck, and I marveled at the happiness of being (well) fed and at once again being immersed in all the sights and colors that my mind was racing to try to remember. The bouncing on the road home did nothing to lessen any of the enjoyment.

THIRTY-SEVEN

IT WAS MIDAFTERNOON. Diego and I sat together outside, enjoying what for many in the world would have been a vacation setting, warm sun, tropical breezes, the scents of flowering topiary transported gently in the air. We are fortunate because this is the atmosphere we generally live in, although we, each in our own locales, get more urban, "civilized", hah, intrusions, exhaust fumes, and other such detractions. He finished filling me in with what he knew, though it was all second hand, about Guzman. They had never done business directly; at least that Diego was sure of. His crew did make a delivery he was pretty sure was directly from his outfit, it was boxes and boxes of, well, the boxes were no heavier than any typical file box, so it could have been documents or it could have been money. The delivery was made, the fee paid, end of that story. Who knows, he says, we do this a lot, maybe other jobs came from him as well, but it isn't a process heavy on record keeping, so who knows, he says with a shrug. They have never gone head-to-head with any business that they were both seeking, he is pretty sure of that. He knows, from the culture he knows so well, that Guzman is involved in drugs and money.

That is without doubt. Gunrunning, that is pretty certain. People smuggling, he doesn't think so, because that would have made it more likely that their paths would have crossed. He also 'knows' that there are many businesses that appear legitimate that are propped up by or are used to launder, the money from the other enterprises. He has been told that Guzman has an entire building somewhere filled with computers and phone lines and low wage operators who spend their whole shifts calling people, looking for those vulnerable enough that he can part from them some or as much money as possible. Perhaps, we are straying now from certainty, that he has many outlets for fraud, from fake documents to fake phone cards to investment swindles, even fake real estate deals and mortgage fraud. But he lives up to his nickname, the shadow, because he seems to be everywhere, but is not fully visible. So, I wonder to myself, what do I think I'm doing? I stepped on his foot. He didn't like it, even if it wasn't a big part of his operation. He came after me, in my own back-yard, but then decided not to. He might stay with that, but then I showed up in Miami. Now what? Should I consider him a threat, or should I report what I've seen, that will make an interesting telling, and let bigger forces than myself decide what to do? It wasn't that hard a question. If I can do something to scramble this guy's operation, I would.

We spent the rest of the afternoon making ready, which consisted of sitting around and each of us thinking our own thoughts.

THIRTY-EIGHT

THE SUNLIGHT was beginning to fade. The ocean was relatively calm, with small waves that would barely raise the bow of the speedboat. Perfect launch conditions, except for the light.

Diego said, "If all goes right, we might get to see the sun actually dip its toes into the waters of the Gulf. I really would prefer more clouds and less light, but …"

If all goes right. Yes, it would be nice to see the sun go down into the water to the west, something that I get to see more often on the west coast than Diego does on the east coast. Try as I might, I was having a hard time thinking about this cruise as a pleasure cruise. I felt pretty tight about it actually.

Some of the men had been looking out, with their binoculars, for some time now. We didn't have to go, if something troublesome appeared, but we did need to go. Okay, enough of that, time to put doubt aside and seize the adventure. I felt partly stronger. Diego and Miguel had been monitoring the conditions. I felt a slight change in the wind—it seemed to be coming ashore just a little bit stronger. The small waves seem to slap a little bit harder. Diego nodded at me, it's time to go. We each thanked Miguel, shook hands, and with 'buen viaje' from Miguel we went out onto the dock. Miguel was coordinating any sign from the lookouts, but there was no impedance in evidence. We entered the stealth boat's hiding place, Diego rolled up the canvas curtain hiding the stern, he loosed the one tie-down, and the engines came softly to life. We left the protective confines of the boat shack, which I felt like anointing the boat palace it had done its job so well. Diego headed the prow into the growing surf, gave a wave to the men on watch and one to Miguel, and we moved slowly, quietly into deepening and darkening water. I had the watch to port. Diego was looking ahead and to starboard. We advanced further and further into our escape. It took some effort to keep my binoculars trained on my watch area, with the boat rising and falling, although relatively gently, but not completely predictable. I did not see anything, but this did not lessen my commitment to looking. I didn't ask, but Diego said, 'soon', perhaps alerting the engines that they were about to engage in heavier duty. It was going okay.

Diego got to the point where he felt a little more power was right. Once again his acceleration was masterful, gentle, no excess noise, but there was greater propulsion. For the first time I turned to face a different direction, cast my gaze all around, then finished the sweep by looking at Diego with a quick up and down of raised eyebrows, and an exhale. He gave a quick 'yes, I know' nod, put a little more power to the screws. I was beginning to turn to my watch area again when we both heard the pop. I turned to look to my right. Diego turned to look at the engines. The engine hum was low and steady, no sign of misfire or other problem. Because I was looking to the right, I caught the next pop, pop first. Diego looked forward.

"From our right," I said.

The pops became less individual and more repetitive. The retort of the weapon fire broadcast itself more sharply through the air than the pulse of engines. We were in twilight and the visibility was decreasing. The first we saw was the prow of a boat, a go-fast boat heading for us. Next came lights, streaming along in the wake of the go-fast. But there were two sets of lights, too widely set to be from the same source.

The go-fast was coming right toward us. Was this a Cuban version of our own coast guard, with their own interceptors to counter the high-powered machinery of smugglers and ner'-do-wells? Looked like we were about to find out. The go-fast saw us, we weren't yet up to real speed and couldn't hit it at this point, we would have likely run right into each other. The other boat's pilot saw us and we could see him give a twist to the wheel and veer off. The three inhabitants of the go-fast looked right at us. It wasn't a Cuban Coast Guard boat. Luis Guzman looked right at me and I at him. He did a quick focus on me, and I, well maybe I imagined he started to say 'whaaat?', but things were happening too quickly to think about that for more than an instant. We had been focusing on the lead boat coming right at us, but when it zoomed past us we saw where the two sets of lights were coming from. A Cuban government patrol boat was almost right behind him, with both its spotlights and a forward gunner trying to pin them down. The other set of lights came from a second patrol boat, running further out and trying to outflank the go-fast while the first patrol boat chased. It seemed Guzman's go-fast might not have quite the speed or power that we had, but nevertheless for the moment was trying to outrun its pursuers. If it turned out to sea the flanker would have easy pickings if it didn't distance itself more. As soon as the go-fast avoided colliding with us, Diego too knew what the situation was. He made a brilliant move. He hit the power, no sense worrying about noise now, and spun the wheel. The boat heeled around close to 270 degrees and as soon as Diego took it out of the turn it practically leapt out of the water and sped the opposite direction of the hare and pursuers. The gunner on the front of the pursuing patrol boat saw us and started to turn his gun, but we jumped out of position so fast he just turned back to forward, and fired. The sound of the weapon so close was rattling. We caught the smell of weapons fire, too, both from these close-by bursts and from previous firings. The trail of smoke from the earlier rounds was only just catching up as we were passing going the other way. I looked back and the go-fast boat's pilot must have caught Diego's move. He tried to copy it. He turned back inside on his path, but since he was, presumably, at full speed, it didn't work out the same. Still, the go-fast had more maneuverability than the patrol boat, and despite the long arc that the go-fast needed in order to turn, he was able to get some separation from the tailing patrol boat. We looked to the flanker, running outside defense. He too was turning, but he turned the opposite direction to try to position himself against the goal line fly pattern.

We were now headed out to the open ocean where the patrol boats had no chance to overtake us. The flanker wouldn't be able to catch us, but his weapons could still reach.

The other go-fast was still mimicking our moves and was gathering steam for a run for the open. I looked at Diego, who had a bead on getting across the goal line first. His eyes just slightly swiveled between his path ahead and the flanker coming across. I shouted, "Diego, we have to do something." He looked at me, and the expression was, 'What do you think I'm doing?!' "We have to cut off Guzman." 'What, why, NO' all tumbled out as fast as the weapons fire. "We must, now! Turn into him!" Diego shook his head a few times then let out a practically anguished 'ahhhggg' and turned the prow. We were losing outgoing distance with our course veer as the other was gaining it. The flanker patrol boat was now bearing down for an interception that might be coincident with a collision, or two. The flanker's forward gunner had been silent but now opened up. A thin scratch went across the otherwise perfect front deck of Diego's boat. 'Shit' Diego screamed, then seemed to bear down harder on a course directly for Guzman. The flanker was coming directly in, aiming at first for the bad guys, but he had two birds rushing toward him. All three occupants of the bad boat saw us coming. Diego's superior speed allowed him to aim right for the go-fast.

Ramming speed, I couldn't help but think to myself. The other go-fast's pilot did not seem to have an answer, he had, after all, been copying all of Diego's moves, and there was no copying this one. We were racing right for them. Collision was imminent. Diego didn't flinch, he kept the hammer down. I braced and waited for the bang this was going to make. The copycat pilot spun away. Salted spray was everywhere. The flanker's gunner fired but didn't hit us again. We powered into the embrace of the ocean and darkness. Behind us, the flanker patrol boat was on Guzman's go-fast, which had practically spun itself into a halt with the inferior pilot's bailout. It made a few engine revs, but kept turning in a circle, almost as if it were already caged. The other patrol boat closed in on them from behind, and we watched the spotlights shine only on a single prize as we ran out of sight.

THIRTY-NINE

WE POWERED ONWARD into the dark of night. We ran without lights because we had no idea whether the patrol boats would call for pursuit or whether somebody would decide on an aerial intervention. Every bound over the waves propelled us to the double-edged sword of U.S. protection and U.S. interdiction. We weren't contending with rain and no-visibility overcast skies either, so it was much more relaxed, though Diego kept a watch, and I did the same. Running into an outsized piece of flotsam could still spoil our dash for the comforts of home. Every once in awhile I would feel Diego looking at me, not the ocean ahead. I would turn and look at him, he would just shake his head side to side like trying to clear a fleeting but unwelcome mental image, and then look ahead again. It wasn't until the third time that he did this that a wry smile finally crossed his face after the head shake. We hadn't spoken, but after our getaway from the patrol boats was accomplished I had given him a clenched fist chest high 'way to go' gesture and nodded my appreciation to him. He merely rolled his eyes and bore his gaze into what there was of a horizon. So, an eye roll, a couple 'man you are nuts looks', then finally a smile. Gripping interaction. We powered on for some time, the rhythm of the forward and back roll of our frames as we pounded through the relatively benign sea our only link. Finally, Diego eased the throttle a bit and made an attempt at standing tall, and then rolling his shoulders, easing the tension of his grip on the wheel. He eased it down to where we could talk, and hear, over the engines.

"That is the closest I have ever been to those patrol boats."

I was pretty sure he was generalizing about those particular patrol boats.

"I have been chased before, but they were never that close."

Then as if he were just remembering, although I think he was just finally allowing himself to say it, "They shot my boat."

I waited to see if there would be more.

He stood silent for a long moment. He then reduced the throttle way down. We still moved forward, but the slow speed increased the pitching of the boat.

"You did a great job."

He stood there shaking his head side to side. Finally he turned to fully face me. "I can't believe you got me to do that."

He didn't mean the escape. That was in the cards. He meant the cut-'em-off at the pass. It worked, I was very happy with it. I was pretty sure that he was struggling with the risk to himself coupled with the now- you're-wearing-a-white-hat action.

He wasn't ready to deal with it. He retreated to a male safety place—we'd talk about logistics.

"I slowed down so we could gather ourselves."

Well, okay, I've been gathered since we were out of sight of the patrol boats.

"I feel pretty safe now."

Well, that did take awhile. Maybe my naiveté at this is over-influencing me.

"We'll hit it again in a moment, but for less than an hour, then we'll have to stop and just wait it out a bit."

Good, give commands, give direction, which always helps recoup confidence, and stabilize one's self.

"Before daylight we can start again. My guys, well, it's best if they come out as if they are with the early morning fishing departures. We'll have enough fuel left to putter around like we're the advance scouts looking for fish for the outcoming paying customers." He looked at me, and was clearly more relaxed. "I've never had to use that excuse, but it is one we've rehearsed."

I smiled the broadest smile that I could muster at him, my best Tom Cruise-ish smile from *Risky Business* and said, "It's a great plan."

Well all-righty then he nodded and put pressure to the throttle. We motored peacefully for the next while.

We held to the schedule set forth. It was quite dark. I wondered, aloud, whether the lights should be on so that we would not be run over by some ship in the night. Great idea, in theory, came the reply, but too vulnerable. Well, sounded like a debate issue, 'Question: is it better to be discovered by a surveillance system, or run over (in the dark, you won't hear it coming, you're going to drown, or, worse)?' I felt our positions switch. I had been calm about the escape, well, actually, I hadn't been calm, I just let go of it sooner, but now I was in a state of unease. Sit here, in this powerful, fast boat, and wait to be run over by some lumbering steamer. Or broadcast our position. I would have opted for the latter. It would have been a tie vote. Tie goes to the captain. Is there a printout of the rules? Diego slumped into the captain's chair. Sleeping sitting up. I could only manage that in business class on airliners, where I really felt I had no control over anything that happened. Yes, I could go first class and have the complete recline, but it seemed a greater expense than value received. I still had a lot of frugality left in me. I laid down on the rear assemblage of cushions. If I'm going to go, it might as well be peacefully at rest. I woke up to the burble of engines. I was pretty sure it had just started. I retook my forward position. Diego said, 'sorry', I'm not sure for what exactly.

"We can start again, I thought the engines would be a good awakening."

My former negative, worrying about being run over by a steamer, thoughts were gone. I must have been tired. I felt refreshed; the spirit of adventure had been renewed in me. "Let's go."

The sun rising out of the ocean is a magnificent sight. The first light pushes the dark higher into the sky then bursts out at the horizon. The sun has returned. Every National Geographic program about ancient peoples will recite how important it was to have a story about the earth being enclosed in darkness while the sun retired into slumber and how the sun's reawakening each day was a special blessing. It remains true today.

The fingers of sunlight that stretch out over the rolls of the ocean waters magically create sparkles all across the surface, little bursts of golden fireworks spreading horizontally. It's like the earth is applauding the new day. I am reminded of what a positive benefit it would be to greet each new day with this feeling of awe and serenity. And that's just the beginning, the show goes on, coloring any clouds gathered to witness the spectacle with hues of gold and pink, their own special anointment for being there to celebrate. The ocean changes from dark to deep green to blue as the light encourages the sky and sea to mirror one another. It is not only a magical sight to behold, the unfolding of the new day sired by the rising sun, but also it imbues a powerful charge to reflect this majesty in the spirit a person carries into the new day.

It was a relaxing beginning. We were powering toward home, at only just a moderate speed. The water was calm so the ride was quite smooth for ocean going. After about forty minutes of this joy ride the radio twerped. It was brief, not coded, but the brevity served to make the message useful almost singularly to the sender and receiver.

"They are getting close," Diego reported.

Shortly we could spot two boats headed toward. They too were proceeding at a moderate pace, nothing out of the ordinary for a morning fishing excursion. With the radio and the binoculars we knew they were our escort. And then we were three. One of the arrivals was one of the walk-arounds that we had been cruising with just, what? It suddenly felt like it had been a week ago, but it wasn't. The other boat had a slightly more business-like appearance, like a cross between an operating fishing outfitter and a cabin cruiser, maybe a dive boat. This was the one that was equipped to serve, as need be, as a refueler. It pulled into position and one of the two men aboard secured their boat to ours, and ours to theirs. Once that was done, the two-man crew set about doing what they obviously knew well how to do.

The other cruiser adjoined us on the other side, and Diego and I transferred to it, then it moved away from the refueling. I wasn't sure whether this was a safety move or just was, because there was no point to create a floating raft with all three together. Diego welcomed his comrade in arms on the other boat then summoned me. Then the fun began. They broke out a cooler with some fresh melon. The cruiser's pilot produced some thermos type containers, Diego smiled and said, 'café au lait pour monsieur', and poured hot milk into two mugs, then the other pilot topped them with still steaming coffee. This day is going just fine. We sat comfortably, then the pilot brought out a basket, literally, a wooden picnic basket, opened the enveloping checkered towel, and we had fresh pastries to choose from. It was my kind of breakfast, but returning to familiarity was contrasted in my mind with the wonderful culturally different experience we had just had yesterday. I was going to try to replicate our Cuban breakfast again, just to encourage my memory's preservation of how pleasant an experience it was. Sitting with our coffees to taste and the bakery goodies, I also thought to myself how much I wanted to visit the island again. It was so picturesque, so full of appealing colors and settings. Maybe I could find an artistically oriented trade mission or whatever the right situation might be for the government to permit the travel. I'm sure the ones that are permitted have a beneficial purpose, but I'm just as sure it's the excuse to get to go to this once exotic land, this one-time huge destination for sun and fun, and less enlightened pleasures. I'm also sure that this island will one day again be a version of paradise.

We had only made it through one cup of coffee before the fuel transfer operation was complete. I thanked Jess, the pilot who brought the catering, Diego and I bundled up some of the fruit and pastries, and the containers of warm milk and coffee, and reboarded his boat. The refueler pushed off and we all began the final push for home port. We didn't travel together, the three boats separated, at times by quite some distance, but it would have taken only minutes to reconvene if the call were necessary. The sun was still rising and its heat sent shimmers over the surfaces. It wasn't long before we encountered other boat traffic, seemingly mostly fishing oriented. We knew we were close when we started seeing other go-fasts dashing across a still portion of water then bouncing and roaring as they encountered waves, mostly produced by the boats themselves. Diego opened it up just for the enjoyment of it. In the sunlight, the extreme speed the boat was capable of was much more realizable than it had been in the dark of night where it was harder to judge how much distance went flying past.

The speed was a thrill, but as we got into more traffic, it had to be lessened. It turned to just motoring our way in and then we were wakeless one more time. The feeling as we moved smoothly toward docking was far less satisfying than the heroic feeling as we began the mystical chase in the rain and dark, and the combined relief and exhilaration of having made our great escape.

I said to Diego, "Do you think we have ended Guzman's criminal empire?"

He started with the now-familiar side-to-side headshake. "I really don't know. I feel like we did, but you made me, remember that."

"C'mon, you know it was right." That was all I was determined to say, to try to intimate that his operation might change too. Yes, it wasn't an overly determined effort on my part.

"Well, he's in a lot of trouble right now, that's for sure." Maybe that would be the best that we could do.

Diego said, "Get the stern line," as we began to dock.

Gee, what a turn of events, he now knew me well enough to trust me with part of the docking. I was actually quite pleased.

With the boat secured, I said to him, "What can I do, I want to pay for the fuel, and I would be honored to pay for getting that scratch fixed."

We'd been through a lot together. It had cost him a considerable amount of money for fuel, if nothing else. He said he got some information that might be useful. Is that it? Was that enough to say 'awh, my treat'?

He looked at the bullet crease across his front deck, then turned to me and said, "You are an honorable guy. That is a very important quality. Thank you for your offer, the fuel, but no, no thank you, no..." He looked back to the scratch. "To tell you the truth, I haven't decided what to do about that yet. I don't like my things to be less than perfect, but, well, I, well, I, I can't help but think maybe I want to be reminded, for now, maybe, about what have, well, about what that scratch could mean. For now."

There was hope for him.

Then he shifted gears, "I want us to do this again," he was moving too fast for himself for a second, "Not Cuba, no. We should get the girls and the boats, this time on a warm sunny afternoon when they can all wear bikinis, that will be good." He laughed. It was a good image to conjure to shake off his reflective moment.

"Count me in."

We shook hands and parted.

FORTY

I WAS IN MY STUDIO in San Isabel working on a painting. I had started this painting a few days ago and had found myself working on it steadily. For these last couple of days, I had started with early mornings on the beach. I would walk a little, right on the edge of the shore, with the water lapping in and curling over my toes and feet then retreating, again and again. Sometimes I sat on the beach and looked out to sea. Sometimes I sat in one of the chairs at the beach restaurant nearby. It was early enough that no one else was around. This time spent both soothed me and then powered me up, sending me with a renewed enthusiasm back to my painting where I worked at it for a couple hours before the steam drained and it was time for a break, to relax, then begin again.

I had followed this routine this morning as well. This felt like a good day. I felt I was closing in on this piece, and I was enjoying the time spent in both contemplation and then action with my brushes and tools and paint.

When it came time for a rest, regroup, recharge break late in the afternoon, I did. I walked the hard edge of the sand where the lapping waves compressed it, then onto the hot, soft sand just beyond, until my feet needed cooling, then back to the gentle water massage again. I sat for a little time on the hot sand and watched the waves form and roll evenly in, giving joy to the many frolicking in the first shallow measure before the ocean became the deep.

I shook my head slightly to shake the reverie, ready to rise up from the sand, prepared to work again. I rose and turned to head in almost in one motion and nearly ran into a woman walking toward the water. A beautiful, long-legged woman. With a tan that was beginning to mature.

"Oh, sorry," I said, then "Hi."

"It's okay" she smiled.

Aim high.

"Say, I live here, and I've seen you on the beach before."

"Oh," she said, but she wasn't hurrying away.

"Are you visiting?"

She looked at me for a moment, she smiled, still not retreating or hurrying on.

"No, I've just moved here."

Nice.

"Could I welcome you with a dinner and some wine?"

"Maybe you could."

The smile remained as she took slow steps toward the water.

"Soon."

She kept walking slowly away but smiled at me with her whole face.

"Yes."

I watched her until she stepped into the water then dived under the incoming small wave. She emerged, looked toward shore, gave me a wave and then stroked further into the sea.

Good, I thought.

An hour later, I remembered for about the fifth time how this had gone. My mind was afloat with things; there was much to contemplate. I wasn't painting for the moment, too much interference in my brain instead of the concentrated calm that worked best for me. I poured myself a cognac and sipped. I walked over to my desk and saw my sheath of notes from this last investigation case. I gathered up the notes and put them into a binder. Perhaps someday my notes would make a good book, I thought. I had another sip of cognac.

A bit of calm returned to my mind. Ah, the power is starting to reignite. There were many positive things in my future and positive thoughts always help drive me to my most productive state. There was this afternoon and the recall, once again, was stoking the fire. Then, I had made plans to go to visit Hig and do some racing. That was a strong positive flow. Also, I have received several communiqués from the acquisitions director of a museum dedicated to contemporary painting in Florence. They have completed some fundraising and were committed to acquiring not one but two of my works. On top of that, they wanted me to be present when the display was to open, so I will be going to Italy. A flow of enthusiasm followed, maybe helped along with the small warm wave of comfort from the drink. I turned back to my painting. Outside the sun had set and twilight was chasing it on its long journey of solaris. The stars that followed in the wake of twilight were beginning to appear. Soon the expanse of water would twinkle with their reflected light and dance with deeper shadows from the clouds that wandered in to accompany the enclosing darkness. There was a lot of black in this painting as well, but not an overwhelming amount. I like black in my paintings, a lot. But Franz Kline still did the sweeps and slashes of white and black best, so far. Perhaps that will change. I added some yellow where I knew it was needed, and some more white, accenting my own sweeps and dashes of primary and secondary colors. I stood back, and with those few touches just applied, I knew. Anything more would start into overworking. I knew. I knew it was finished, and I was ready. I picked up a small stiff bristled brush and in the lower right corner stroked in A B Black.

ABOUT THE AUTHOR

SCOTT PRICE writes, walks, bikes, skis and thinks.

For inspiration all Scott needs is the morning sunrise, or to view a Franz Kline abstract.